The Eagle's Feather

by William Campbell Douglass

A Novel

Rhino Publishing, S.A.

The Eagle's Feather

Copyright © 1966, 2003
by

William Campbell Douglass, MD

ISBN 9962-636-40-X

Illustrations by J. E. Towery
Cover illustration by
Alex Manyoma (alex@3dcity.com)

Please, visit Rhino's website for other publications from
Dr. William Campbell Douglass
www.rhinopublish.com

Dr. Douglass' "Real Health" alternative medical newsletter is available at www.realhealthnews.com

RHINO PUBLISHING, S.A.
World Trade Center
Panama, Republic of Panama
Voicemail/Fax
International: + 416-352-5126
North America: 888-317-6767

DEDICATION

To those thousand of patriots who are working diligently, day and night, to cause this book to remain fiction.

ACKNOWLEDGMENTS

Without the advice and criticism of the following friends and supporters this book would have been finished much sooner — but never Published:

Harv, Frank C., Mrs. Murphy, Kent, Lynne, June, Earl, Joe, Marie, LaDene, many many others, and.... Phoebe with her merciless blue pencil.

The author.

Although *The Eagle's Feather* is a work of fiction set in the 1970's, it is built, as with most fiction, on a framework of plausibility and background information. A modification of the "telephone grapevine," mentioned in this book, exists today in the form of Dr. Douglass' "Let Freedom Ring!" — the anti-Communist telephone network.

Dr. Douglass insists that all the characters are fictional.

TABLE OF CONTENTS

The shaft of the arrow had been feathered
with one of the eagle's own plumes.

We often give our enemies the means of our
own destruction.

THE EAGLE AND THE ARROW
Aesop - Circa 550 B.C.

UNITED STATES POST O
EL PAS
UNO

1. Dateline El Paso

The victory party for Warren Silverbright, soon to be Florida's new Senator, was less than four hours away and Beth Huckins was feeling the pressure of time. Camelia had not yet done the floors nor polished the silver. The children were being impossible -- as was their custom whenever the Huckinses planned a party. Dr. Huckins' offer to help had been turned down by his wife, with pointed hints from both her and Camelia that he simply keep from getting underfoot. He had retreated to his favorite chair in the living room.

"Dwight, did you get the ice?" Beth called from the kitchen. Her methodical fingers were rapidly turning out small sandwiches with a slice of olive on top. These were added to the great mounds of multi-colored canapes already piled on the carving counter.

Dwight Huckins laid the SARASOTA FLORIDA TIMES carefully on the living room table, almost as if he expected it to explode. "Yes,

Beth," he said absently. Lighting a cigarette he gazed out at the languid Gulf of Mexico, his jaw tightening as he remembered with disgust yesterday's headline. El Paso, Texas, had cancelled its Fourth of July parade "in order to avoid any incidents or embarrassments." The Civil Liberties League had protested the parade on the grounds that the celebration offended alien minorities. And now *this* news! He turned, stared at the explosive headline, then picked up the paper again and read:

CHINESE ENTER EL PASO

United Nations International News Service, July 4, 1970 --

Informed sources reported today that units of the Chinese People's Army have crossed into the United States near Juarez and El Paso, Texas. An unidentified Army officer from White Sands Proving Ground said that elements of the Chinese Army had been seen in downtown El Paso but they appeared friendly and had been orderly. Some had been seen joking with young girls and giving candy to curious children. The same source stated that the report of 80,000 Chinese troops across the Rio Grande was a gross exaggeration.

In an interview with General Otto Swindler, Commanding General, SWAPO (The United Nations' Southwest Army Peace Organization), the General said, "I am not quite sure what my responsibilities are at this time. The situation has parallels with the occupation of Birmingham last year. There, you will recall, the Genocide

Treaty was invoked because of racial hatred of the white majority against the negro minority. In this case **it** is white against yellow." General Swindler ~aid that he was awaiting instructions from SWAPO headquarters in Mexico City.

Chairman Ivan Prusakova of the USSR, the article went on to relate, defended the right of the Chinese People's Army to investigate racial discrimination and, from the UN presidium, had called for United Nations occupation of El Paso.

Huckins looked away from the offensive thing in his hands and back to the ceiling-to-floor window that framed his favorite scene: the snow-white sand of Crescent Beach and the placid Gulf of Mexico with its tiny, lapping waves at the shoreline -- creating a subtropical tranquility that never failed to lift his depressed spirits. The Gulf was a huge bowl of blue-green oil. The wind-driven chattering of the coconut palm fronds had ceased. It was a still, soporific afternoon, so often enjoyed on Florida's west coast in midsummer.

If only he could influence Silverbright, he could help stop this piecemeal surrender of the United States, he thought. Having just won the primary election with a two-to-one majority, Warren Silverbright was expected to have an easy victory in November. Because the opposition was disorganized and split into bitter factions, "Silver" would certainly be a walk-in.

Dwight started as he read the last paragraph of the article:

"Samuel Yen, Director of the UN Reset-
tlement Commission for the SWAPO area,
said that 20,000 Chinese were now reset-
tled in El Paso County and racial prejudice
against the Chinese had become a considerable problem."

Huckins raced through his mental catalogue of names and faces -- a large catalogue
born of his years in Washington in the Navy Department. Sam Yen -- a shiny yellow face and a
glabrous scalp to match; a lot of big teeth and a
head that was forever bobbing up and down in
agreement. The little Chinaman had had the
largest wholesale fur business on the Pacific
Coast. Robert Bliss of the State Department had
brought him to Washington as an assistant. Yen
soon had his fingers into everything. In fact,
Huckins recalled, Yen had been found with his
fingers in some very interesting places, so much
so that Senator Renault had called for an investigation of Yen's activities. The very next day Yen
had suddenly been appointed to SWAPO
thereby conveniently gaining "diplomatic immunity." Huckins threw down the paper con-
temptuously as he recalled that sordid history.
"Diplomatic immunity along with all the other
traitors in the UN," he muttered to himself.

He blew a large cloud of smoke and tossed
the hardly used cigarette among many others in
a large ashtray. Dr. Huckins had a prominent
sharp nose, deep-set, dark blue eyes, and gray
temples; he was tall and well built --not a handsome man but one classified by most women as
"nice looking.'

"Dwight," said Beth behind him, "will you please forget about Texas long enough to get this party over with ?" Sensing that she had irritated him she added, "I'm sorry, darling. I know it's serious. I'm ready to sit down a minute. The children have finally gone out to play with the Blackwoods, and everything's at least under control, so why don't we have a drink?"

Beth took off her shoes and sat on the couch, her feet curled under her. "And the next time we're the party committee," she sighed, "let's volunteer someone else's house."

Dwight poured the drinks pensively, unable to stop thinking about the Texas situation. "Will our forces take a stand?" he wondered. "Our forces? Could this goulash army be called 'ours'? What was the Supreme Commander's name? -- Nyng Yet, or something like that."

His wife interrupted his thoughts as if reading his mind. "Did you see that picture of Nug Tep, or whatever-his-name is, in the NEW TIMES yesterday?" Beth's corn-yellow hair bounced as she talked. "If that man is General Swindler's boss in Area Four, I want to move to Area One *Hundred* and Four -- why he looks like a Chinese toenail puller!" Huckins was mildly irritated by the flippancy of her remark combined with the hard truth it might contain. Who had appointed that filthy-looking character? No one seemed to know where these people came from .

Dwight at first did not reply to his wife's grim humor but lit another cigarette and blew a big puff of thick, uninhaled smoke at a fly on the plate glass window. "It's amazing," he said, as he tried to redirect the conversation, "how modern sanitation has changed the fly from a terrible harbinger of disease and pestilence to a fairly harmless household pest. But let civilization break down and the harmless fly will again become a carrier of death and misery along with the rat, the flea and the louse."

Camelia, overhearing his remark, charged into the living room and attacked the insect with a fly swatter. "He may be harmless, Dr. Dwight, but he isn't coming to *this* party!" Gingerly balancing her dead victim on the fly swatter, she returned to the kitchen.

Beth couldn't resist a smile at the rather clumsy attempt of Dwight's to change the subject. She studied her troubled husband. If he would only accept defeat, perhaps they could live out what was left to them in relative peace. But she knew he never would. He was one of the breed of patriots who would never give up. He often quoted Xenophon, the people whose aim is to keep alive usually find a wretched and dishonorable death; while the people who, realizing that death is the common lot of all men, make it their endeavor to die with honor, somehow seem more often to reach old age and have a happier life when they are alive."

This was Dwight Huckins, M.D. Beth knew that she could not change him and she had stopped trying. Perhaps they would pull America back together. She had always allowed herself this one morsel of hope. One couldn't live with a dedication such as her husband's unless one did. Dwight was a gentle man and, in spite of his patriotic fervor, she could never picture him storming a barricade or killing anyone -- even for his beloved and terribly enervated America. No, she decided, he was not the soldier Xenophon so much as the statesman Demosthenes. Dwight often quoted him too, when criticizing the government's appeasement policies.

Two years ago, when they had been a part of Washington, he had said at a meeting of top Navy brass, "'You make war like a barbarian when he wrestles ... if he suffers a blow he immediately puts his hand to it. If he is struck again, he puts his hand *there*. But he has not the skill to evade his antagonist . . . . Never a fixed plan! Never any precautions! You wait for bad news before you act!' Demosthenes was talking to the Greeks, gentlemen, but it sounds as though he was talking to you!"

The Navy Department had taken a dim view of the doctor's outspoken criticism. His superior suggested that he stick to his pills. When the missile cruiser LITTLE ROCK was torpedoed, and the Navy refused to investigate because the unified crew of foreigners from eight different countries made it "a UN problem," Dwight had said that he couldn't be a part of a military organization which would tolerate the sinking of one of its own vessels. He had resigned his commission in disgust and returned to Sarasota.

Beth sipped her highball, then set it on the coffee table and leaned back on the divan. "I understand Carla is coming to the party with that new bachelor dermatologist."

Dwight smiled. "Are you jealous?"

"Of course I'm jealous," she replied quickly. "She tried to hook you before and she certainly isn't the type to let a little thing like a marriage stand in her way. She's awfully clever, you know."

"It's amazing," he countered, "how much you women think alike. You all seem to believe that men are helpless pawns, completely at the mercy of designing women."

Beth detected the subtle flash of annoyance in his eyes. "Well, aren't some of them?" she compromised.

Dwight sat down beside her and looked into her eyes. "Mrs. Huckins, if Carla approached me in the most tantalizing negligee imaginable, with a million dollars in one hand and a bottle of champagne in the other, do you think I would betray you?"

Beth put her arms around her husband and kissed his ear. "No, darling, I know you wouldn't."

Dwight had won his argument. Beth had planned it that way.

The telephone rang and Camelia answered it in the kitchen. "It's the nurse in the Intensive Care Ward, Dr. Dwight. She's calling about Mrs. Clark."

"Probably hematemesis again," he said as he crossed the room. "This is the third time this year she's bled from her duodenal ulcer and I'd like Jim MacDonald to do a gastrectomy if I could get her into shape."

Beth loved to have her husband talk about his cases in medical terms although she often didn't understand the words and knew few of his patients. She never interrupted his chain of thought by asking for explanations. Dwight liked to "think out loud" because it helped him formulate his plans and make decisions.

He picked up the receiver. "Hello, yes, Mrs. Houston ... I was afraid of that. Type her for four more units of blood and start it as soon as you can. Put down a nasogastric tube and after you have suctioned out the blood, lavage her stomach with some ice water -- I'll be right in." He slammed down the receiver, kissed his wife and grabbed his coat in one continuous maneuver. "Chin up, sweetheart, I'll be home in time for the party."

Beth was long accustomed to these disruptions and had learned never to let Dwight's sudden departures disturb her. "I'll feed the children ahead," she said. Dwight was halfway out the front door. "Call me if you get tied up. Remember, the party starts at seven." He promised that he would, and his car was soon roaring out of the driveway into the winding road that led to the main highway to Sarasota.

Dr. Huckins wove in and out of the fourlane traffic. He knew the run to the hospital better than his own backyard. He referred to his Buick convertible as "trail broke" and considered it almost capable of making the trip by itself. His mind could reflect independently of his driving. "I don't think Mrs. Clark is going to make it," he mused. "Her age and her cirrhosis are certainly against her." He soon spun the convertible into the doctors parking area, and the nose of the car dipped as he brought it to an abrupt halt. "But I don't suppose anyone but the doctor is going to worry about Mrs. Clark's liver with the Mongols entering El Paso.~, Grabbing his stethoscope from the rear seat, he checked in with Doctors' Answering Service on his automobile radio-telephone and headed for the Intensive Care Ward.

2. Warren Silverbright

Warren Silverbright had the look of an eighteen-year-old boy with curly steel-gray hair. He was unusually tall; his posture poor. His upper teeth were prominent, adding to his adolescent appearance. Silverbright and Dwight Huckins had become acquainted at college when they had played varsity football together. Other than being teammates and the fact that they were both from Florida, they had little in common. Dwight loved classical music, good liquor in moderation and a long cigar. Warren was an ardent jazz fan. He neither smoked nor drank; both made him sick. Huckins was Protestant; Silverbright Jewish. As with most things in life, Huckins took his religion seriously. Warren Silverbright saw nothing serious about religion or anything else, and he lived his life accordingly.

After college their paths had diverged. Huckins went on to medical school while Silverbright returned to Bradenton, Florida, to work in his father's brokerage firm. By the time Huckins had completed his internship five years later, Silverbright was deeply involved in State politics. The fight for State Representative of Manatee County, adjoining Sarasota County, was the most vicious in the area's history. Silverbright's opponent called him, "the playboy son of a wealthy stockbroker," which was exactly what he was. Silverbright called his opponent, "a cocky woolhat know-nothing who wants to feed at the public trough," which was exactly what he was.

The campaign was considered a tossup by both sides until "the Jewish issue" was raised, not by Silverbright's opponent, but by Silverbright's campaign manager and younger brother, Robbie. Robbie Silverbright quietly organized six of Warren's supporters and had them make anonymous telephone calls to selected gullible citizens, telling them that Silverbright was part of a dark Zionist plot to take over the world. They would terminate their call with, "We Christians must drive these dirty Jews out before it's too late!" Then they would hang up. One call was to a local columnist who prided himself on his fairness and lack of racial prejudice.

The columnist received "evidence" of the anti-Semitic campaign from his friends and swallowed the bait whole. His next column was headed, "Anti-Semitism Shames Our County." It broke the election wide open. The people rushed to the polls to prove their non-prejudice and Warren Silverbright won handily.

Warren and Dwight might never have met again had not diabetes struck Silverbright and brought him to the emergency room of the Sarasota Memorial Hospital. Silverbright was in Sarasota vacationing, following his successful bid for the Florida House of Representatives. He had had a cold for two weeks and had ignored it during the busy campaign. He had attributed his peculiar symptom complex of abdominal pain, insatiable thirst, lethargy, headache and nausea to his neglected cold. He was found lying before his motel door at ten o'clock one evening, semi-comatose and delirious.

Dr. Huckins had the emergency room duty that night and immediately recognized Silverbright when the ambulance driver wheeled him in on the stretcher. "Looks like another drunk tourist, Dr. Huckins," the driver said.

Dwight's more practiced eye recognized something far more serious. He noticed that the patient's breathing was deep and slow -- possibly representing the Kussmaul breathing of diabetic acidosis. He immediately felt Warren's eyeballs through his closed eyelids. Were they soft as in diabetic acidosis? It was hard to tell. Silverbright was obviously dehydrated and he was mumbling incoherently. Dwight ordered an emergency blood sugar and intravenous fluids. He smelled Warren's breath and then the diagnosis was certain. The characteristic fruity smell of diabetic acidosis was clearly evident.

It took two days of carefully supervised intensive treatment to pull Warren through. He proved to be an extremely unstable diabetic, teetering constantly between too much insulin with consequent shock and too little insulin resulting in a return of acidosis. Realizing that Dwight had saved his life, Silverbright insisted on having him for his regular physician, even though it meant a 25-mile-round trip from Bradenton for his checkup every fortnight. When the legislature was in session, he would even fly from the capitol in Tallahassee every other weekend for his appointment.

Dwight had always taken an active interest in politics because he felt it was his duty. In general, he disliked and distrusted professional politicians, but by the time Warren Silverbright ran for the U.S. Senate, Dwight had developed considerable influence in the local party. He worked hard for Silverbright during the campaign, not because he felt that his patient was such a desirable candidate but simply because Warren's opponent represented all the evil forces that Dwight had been fighting against: the Labor union cartels, the invisible government of big business interests wanting to protect their government guaranteed monopolies, and even the Communist Party itself, whose Florida organization had come out openly for him. It was also known that the United Nations had dumped huge sums of money into the campaign coffers of Warren's opponent.

Silverbright was elected to the Senate in November by a narrow margin. The people resented UN intrusion into the Florida campaign.

This, combined with the Communist issue which campaign manager Robbie Silverbright had exposed aggressively and effectively, provided the margin for victory.

Little did the people know, including Dwight Huckins, that the man they had elected on an anti-United Nations, anti-Communist platform would soon propose the most fantastic betrayal in American history: the 26th parallel compromise or "Silverbright Doctrine" as it came to be known. This proposal would earn him the undying hatred of the majority of Floridians. Warren Silverbright's attitude was a classic example of the unprincipled politician's: abandon those who put you where you are if thereby you can appeal to the greed, the ignorance or the cowardice of a larger group.

3. Carla

Carla was more female than most women. Her sexual emotions were on the surface and quickly stimulated. A tan, well-muscled male arm affected Carla as well-formed female hips affect a man. She was a combination of extreme sophistication and sexual primitivity. When talking to a new-found romantic interest, her beautiful white face in its square frame of straight, glossy black hair would flush; her pupils would dilate and even her breasts would seem to take a hopeful and expectant tilt upward. She had the face and body of twenty-five; she was forty-two.

Carla was a sexual athlete and she had a penchant for highly illuminated sex play. She said that if a man was worth making love to he was worth watching, and the more light the better. Sex has always played an important part in the destiny of nations. The phenomenon did not begin with Cleopatra nor end with Catherine the Great. But in Cleopatra's and Catherine's day, photography did not plague the secret lover and entrap him by blackmail. Carla's sexual proclivities would make blackmail easy through highly detailed photographs. This was to have devastating effects on her country, her friends and herself.

Carla had set out in conquest of Dwight Huckins when they were high school classmates. Having failed in her sexual efforts, she had told him, when they were eighteen, that he was "the best candidate for middle age I have ever met." Their romance, if it could be called such, ended quickly and from then on they were polite when they met but not cordial. Carla could never forgive him entirely, for she was not accustomed to defeat. As for Dwight, he was contemptuous of Carla because of her moral turpitude, although as a man he admired her beauty and sophistication.

The party at the Huckinses' home in July, celebrating the primary election victory of Warren Silverbright, started a concatenation of events that would lead many of those present to the White House. The incident that triggered this chain of events was Huckins' introduction of Silverbright, flushed with victory, to the petite Carla. Warren's casual attitude toward life and his unstable diabetic condition made him a poor risk at any endeavor, and he was certainly unfit for the Presidency. The woman he was about to meet would drive him there.

Warren Silverbright was not ordinarily an aggressive suitor, but this night was his --and one victory leads to another. Gazing contempla-tively over his ginger ale glass, it was obvious that he was absorbed in Carla and oblivious to the sound of celebrants filling the living room. "Say, Doctor, who is the doll dressed in the black hair and the well formed you-know-whats?"

Dwight studied his guest with amusement. Carla would have the big lug at her knees within twenty-four hours if she so desired. "That, Mr. Senator, is Carla and, as a matter of fact, she's between husbands." Warren's eyes had not left the trim little figure across the room. Her simple black dress accentuated the concavities of her small, firm buttocks. She turned toward Warren as a woman will when her female instinct sig-nals that an admirer is on a collision course. Her green eyes met his. Dwight, observing this, sighed resignedly and set his Martini glass on the table. "Senator, I must warn you, this girl is quite a handful."

Silverbright resisted the temptation to make a pun, accepted a fresh glass of ginger ale from a waiter and said, "Wonderful, let's go!" They crossed the room together. Dwight felt that he was leading a sheep to the slaughter -- and so he was. He introduced Warren to Carla and im-mediately became excess baggage. Excusing himself, without being heard by either of them, he retired a distance to observe. He smiled with amusement as he watched the towering, rather juvenile figure of Warren Silverbright bent al-most into the shape of a question mark, talking earnestly to the cool, erect, calculating Carla. As Warren sipped his drink, Carla contemplated the hairs on the back of his large, masculine fingers. Her chemistries began to work. Carla's conquest was well under way...

Silverbright had never really wanted any woman with an all-consuming passion. If a girl discouraged him, even slightly, it was typical of Warren to drop from the contest. But from that first night he decided that he must have Carla and he threw himself into the project with a ferocity that amazed his friends. It was largely unnecessary, for Carla had made her decision that night too. She had decided that they would be married in three months. That would leave time for a honeymoon before moving to Washington in November to get settled before the opening of Congress in January.

For the first two weeks following the party, Carla managed to be seen practically everywhere with every eligible male in town --everyone but Silverbright. Wherever he went, Warren saw her. He called her apartment at least twice a day, but she was never home. He didn't quite have the nerve to call late at night, but finally, screwing up his courage, he did call her early one morning.

"Hello ?" The sleepy voice at the other end gave away what he feared would be his first mistake of the day.

"I'm sorry if I awakened you, Carla."

"Who is this?" There was a shade of annoyance in her voice.

"It's Warren Silverbright."

"Oh?" Her voice was flat.

Warren fought back panic. "I know it's a strange time to call but ... well, I've called you a number of times and...

"Is there something urgent? I mean *really*, Warren--it's 7:30 in the *morning*."

He was adrift, paralyzed, mortified. "I'm sorry -- really I am. But I couldn't reach you and I only..

Carla impaled her prey. "Well, it's awfully early but I don't really mind." Her voice was suddenly warm and friendly. "Are you coming downtown this morning?"

The words tumbled out: "I wasn't ... I mean I can.., that is if lean do anything..."

"Well, come on down and I'll fix you some burned toast and coffee -- that is, if you can come." Warren mumbled something unintelligible, hung up and dashed for his car.

During the next few weeks, Silverbright stumbled and careened from one romantic crisis to another. He fretted and worried about Carla's other male friends, but by the fourth week of the pursuit he was monopolizing most of her time and only one persistent suitor stood in his way.

Finally, Carla was ready for the kill. One afternoon, as they were having lunch at a sidewalk restaurant she announced, "Warren, I won't be able to see you next week end. Bob has asked me to go to Miami." Warren's mouth fell open and his eyes bulged a little. "His family is having a reunion and he wants me to meet his father."

Warren dropped his sandwich. "To hell with Bob's father. You're marrying me!" He grasped her hand across the table, suddenly contrite. "I mean, will you? Please, Carla, don't go. I couldn't stand it."

Carla put her other hand over his. "All right, darling, I won't go. I don't like Miami anyway."

"But will you?" he persisted.

"But will I what?"

"Will you marry me?"

She smiled and blew smoke in his face. "Not today I won't."

Warren, his lunch forgotten, pressed on. "Well, when will you?" He clutched her hand. "Please give me an answer, Carla. I love you so much. I have to know!"

"Well, I don't like Miami, but I do like Washington..."

Warren quickly picked the idea up, as if it were his own. "Then we'll get married just before I leave for Washington -- and have our honeymoon on the way up!"

Carla set down her glass. "Darling, you just bought yourself a lifelong problem. Take me out of here and kiss me."

Warren quickly signed the check and they left. Pride welled within him. Carla was his! Over insuperable obstacles he had conquered!

Because of Carla's well-known and highly checkered past, news of their courtship spread rapidly. "With her reputation it will ruin his career," was the typical comment. Nothing could have been farther from the truth. Although Carla's reputation for having an appetite for men did not improve as a Senator's wife -- and for good reason --she began working successfully toward the White House the day she and Warren were married. Her extra-marital affairs seemed not to matter; although women hated her, they would do her bidding. The men, of course, were easy.

A week after they arrived in Washington, the new junior Senator from Florida and his beautiful bride were guests at the White House. The President, a widower of two years, was short, somewhat overweight and bald except for snow-white hair around the base of his pink scalp. Since the First Lady's death, his older sister, Helen, had taken over as official hostess. The President was immediately taken with Carla. Helen was not.

"Tell me, Mr. President," Carla handed him another Scotch and soda, "what do you think of Dr. Brosnev's allegations against the United States in South America?" Her breasts tilted upward expectantly. Helen was fidgeting about, trying to regain control of an obviously dangerous situation.

"Now, Carla, honey," the Scotch was warming the President's blood, "why should you worry your pretty little head over things like that?"

Carla had learned to use directness as a shock weapon: "Because I want to help my husband. I want him to become President of the United States." She carefully flicked a cigarette ash from the President's lapel with a well manicured fingernail, "and I want you to help me." When Carla had her male animal cornered, she would suddenly turn to stone, fix her victim with her emerald eyes and wait. The President was thoroughly transfixed.

He caught his breath, flushed and said, "You're quite a girl, aren't you?" She did not reply and continued to mesmerize him. The President took a long pull on his Scotch and soda, tore his gaze from Carla's and scanned the room, landing on the tall, stooped figure of Senator Warren Silverbright. He pretended to study the young Senator, but he was still seeing Carla's snow-white face. His mind raced, and he felt an exhilaration that had long been forgotten. "What an entrancing woman," he thought, "what a face -- such charm and dynamism!" He turned back to the exciting creature at his side. "We'll see what we can do, Carla. What committee assignments has he been promised?" In spite of himself, his eyes dropped to the deep "V" on Carla's dress.

Her respirations deepened subtly and held him. "Agriculture and Finance, last we heard. But," she continued pointedly, "it wasn't definite." And to keep him off balance, she added, "Would you light my cigarette?"

Helen's voice, though soft, crashed between them.

"John, you have a terribly long day tomorrow and it starts at eight with the Cabin meeting." Carla smiled sweetly. Her night work was done.

4.　The Yen Family

Mrs. Frisbee, on her annual world tour, had returned to Hong Kong and was again buying a new fur coat. She shook a fur cape with an experienced snap of the wrist, laid it over her elephantine thighs, and carefully caressed it with the palm of her fat hand. "What in hell has happened to the Russian mink?" she exclaimed in her rough, whiskey voice. "They feel like they've been dipped in glue."

Sam Yen was accustomed to Mrs. Frisbee and her vulgarities. Although she pretended to be very rich, he suspected that she sold her new coat every year immediately on returning to Seattle. She always traveled third class and probably paid for her trip through such manipulations. His smooth Chinese face and fixed grin did not reveal his contempt for this repulsive and overbearing woman. The mink with its beautiful sheen looked even richer in contrast to the gaudy purple, pink and white flowered dress worn by the corpulent Mrs. Frisbee.

"We thought they were somewhat better this year, Mrs. Frisbee. Let's try this one on."

Finally satisfied, after trying on almost every coat in the shop, Mrs. Frisbee strode out of the store, her purchase in a box under her arm. Sam Yen looked after her and made his annual remark about Mrs. Frisbee to his wife. "There's another $5,000 for the Party and it won't even hide her fat ankles much less her ugly, fat, capitalistic American face."

Sam Yen had always been a merchant, and he had always been a Communist Party member. Before the Yens came to Hong Kong in 1951, their food shop in Chungking had been a center for Communist agents from all over the world. The storeroom over the shop was seldom without activity. Messages were sent to and received from Berlin, Moscow, Tokyo and Hawaii every day. Much coding and decoding and interminable cell meetings took place in the storeroom. The crude printing press was rarely idle.

When Chiang Kai-Shek was retreating from the Red Chinese in 1948, the Yen store became a beehive of action and all pretense at secrecy was dropped. Yen's headquarters played a key part in Chiang's defeat. The scheme that sounded the death knell to Chiang's army had been born among the cases of tea and rice in Yen's upstairs storeroom.

The man from Washington, Abbott Z. Larrimore, always immaculate in dress, bespectacled with heavy horned rims, and professorial in appearance, had come to the Chungking shop. He had asked Sam Yen what he thought could be done to destroy Chiang Kai-Shek. "Yen, our plan needs the Oriental touch." He sat on a packing case, crossed his legs and caressed his moustache with his little finger.

Sam Yen had reasoned that Chiang could not be destroyed until the sources of his power were destroyed: the support of the Chinese people themselves; and, equally important, Chiang's backing from the United States of America. He had recommended (1) a soft-pedalling of the Communist attack against the Chinese family unit and (2) stopping or misdirecting the flow of ammunition from America at some crucial moment. Yen felt that the ammunition could not be stopped at the source without exposing highly placed agents within the U.S. State Department. It could be accomplished, he had suggested, by *misdirection* of the vital supplies. At a decisive moment in the war an agent in the Congress, posing as a Conservative, would call for immediate, massive aid to Chiang. The tens of thousands of rounds of ammunition would then be rushed to Sam Yen's dingy little store ... and turned over to the Chinese Communist Army.

"Yes, indeed," Larrimore had said. He removed his horn-rimmed glasses and laid them on a packing crate after first carefully blowing away the dust. His faultlessly pressed pin stripe suit contrasted sharply with the dusty clutter in Sam Yen's storeroom. "Yes, your acumen, considering your limited experience, is remarkable. However, not having served in Washington, you don't realize the degree of security our agents enjoy. Your concern about exposure of our people is overdrawn."

Sam Yen hated Larrimore and his patronizing attitude, but his unlined face and perpetual grin masked his irritation. He inwardly laughed at these arrogant, effeminate American Communists because he outranked them all ... and they didn't even know it! Not yet. When the battle was won, they would hang these fools first.., on the White House lawn. In his cunning Oriental way, Yen made maximum use of these State Department fops.

"Yes. Yours will be our basic plan, Yen." Larrimore picked up his glasses and wiped them with an immaculate white handkerchief. "However, that ammunition will never leave the United States." He smiled smugly at Yen who looked down at the floor, feigning disappointment. "I realize that sending all that ammunition to you would increase your stature in the local party apparatus but that isn't really the most important consideration, now is it?"

"No, no, Mr. Larrimore, I only thought.. ."

"Forget it, Yen," he interrupted as he got up to leave. "We know what we are doing and we aren't taking any chances of a double cross at this end. As you know, there are many double agents in Chungking and anything could happen. But don't misunderstand me, we do trust *you.* I have had you thoroughly investigated, Yen, and we have great hopes for you."

"Thank you, Mr. Larrimore. I am deeply honored."

Sam Yen watched as Abbott Larrimore drove off in his State Department limousine. "Yes," he chuckled, "I will take great pleasure in hanging him personally." Sam knew the ammunition would leave the United States, but would never reach Chiang Kai-Shek's forces. It would simply be dumped into the sea. Total valuation: $150,000,000.

Tremendous events transpired soon after that meeting. Chiang Kai-Shek was driven off the mainland to Formosa, and China fell to Communist slavery. The only real threats to Communist expansion in the Far East, Generalissimo Chiang Kai-Shek and General MacArthur, were effectively neutralized by Communist operatives within the American government.

Two years later, the Yen family, father, mother, and young son, arrived in Hong Kong in a Chinese junk, clothed in rags and half-starved. They appeared no different from untold thousands of others who were fleeing the horrors of Communism. The Yens did well in Hong Kong after their "escape" from the mainland, as well they should.., the Communist Party had staked them with $100,000.

In their twelve years of retailing in Hong Kong, mostly Russian mink, the Yen's Manchurian Fur Shop had built a solid reputation.

American contacts had been carefully made and carefully catalogued. The news of their fabulous bargains had spread to all corners of the globe and almost every person of means stopped in the Manchurian Fur Shop on his trip to the Orient. Sam and his wife, Ling, sent Christmas cards every year with carefully written notes to each American customer. They had laid their plans well over the years and the San Francisco shop, a perfect cover for espionage operations in America, would be opened soon. Eighteen-year-old Charles, their son, would go to the University of California at Berkeley. As a refugee and "expert" on Chinese Communism, he could serve well and add further respectability and credence to the family situation.

Ling and Charles Yen had always helped Sam in any way they were instructed. They asked no questions about his activities and frequent trips, especially during the Korean war, and were not expected to. When the family left for San Francisco in 1963, wife and son knew only that Sam Yen was a highly trusted member of the international conspiracy to which they all swore allegiance. Sam Yen was indeed highly trusted: he was a full colonel in the Soviet Secret Police.

5. 26th Parallel

When the grooming of Warren Silverbright for the presidency started in the winter of 1975, he was almost unknown outside Florida, and had served only five years of his six-year term. However, the right committee assignments, his backing by unions and the big foundations, and a carefully planned image build up by newspapers and television soon turned him into "the indispensable man." The opinion polls, which had not even listed Silverbright before the primaries, found him in the summer of 1976 to be the favorite of "52.7% of the voters and trending upward."

Big Labor boss Charlie Rubio, sat before Senator Silverbright's desk. Rubio had no neck. His large, greasy head was attached to huge rounded shoulders by the fat that rolled over his collar like a giant doughnut. His cigar never left his mouth. Cigar ashes were seldom absent from his shirt and the area around him.

"Silverbright, your job is simple." He pointed a pudgy finger, its nail carefully polished, at the Senator. "Give the unions hell but vote union. Praise free enterprise, but keep the bastards nailed to the wall. Businessmen are cowards except for rare exceptions. Not only are they cowards, but they can't see beyond tomorrow's profits. Name your price for the campaign and if they balk, promise them a few more nails in their coffin." Another big ash dropped onto his tie and bounced to the rug. "Every damned one of them will kick in, thinking that his contribution will save *him* while we flatten the others.

The "we" in Rubio's dialogue was irritating. Silverbright wondered, who was going to run for President anyway? The room was hazy blue from the cigar smoke and the Senator was feeling a vague nausea, partly from the smoke and partly from a feeling of entrapment -- the entrapment and disgust one feels when he has gone beyond the point of no return with an evil force over which he has no control. He started to interrupt, but Rubio continued.

"You just keep your nose clean, and clear your statements with me and Sidney and you'll be in the driver's seat next year." Rubio, squat and swarthy, stood up abruptly, put on his hat and lumbered toward the door. "I got a meeting -- my best to your missus --she's a real dish."

The Senator got to his feet and hurried around his desk to pat Rubio on his massive back. "I'll tell Carla you dropped in, Charlie.

Give my best to Pearl." Rubio grunted assent and disappeared in a cloud of smoke.

Senator Silverbright slumped into the leather chair recently occupied by Charlie Rubio. It was still warm from his massive rump. Silverbright jumped up, revolted by the familiarity with the fat man that the sensation engendered. He turned up the air conditioner to clear out the smoke and settled back into his own chair behind his glass-covered desk. Tapping a pencil on the desk top, he reviewed the last hour's ordeal. He was in deep with these hoodlums, but the goal certainly required some compromises. Carla wanted him to be President; this was the way.

Carla also despised the fat man, but they needed his power. She had helped Warren rationalize the alliance with Rubio. "After all," she had said, "Roosevelt stretched the truth and played Conservative to get in. We'll play left and, once we are in, we can dump Rubio, the Communists and all the rest of those creeps. They control the *money*, darling. It's the only way." She pressed close to her troubled husband. "Why don't we take a nap?"

After their love-making, guilt flooded back over Senator Silverbright. What would Dwight Huckins and his other Florida supporters think? He knew that Huck would consider his coalition with Rubio a betrayal and he could never tell him.

Because of his constantly unpredictable diabetes, he needed Dwight's help. The public was to be kept ignorant of Silverbright's disease and a physician would have to be on constant call to keep the condition under control. He feared that the information would leak to the public if he used a succession of different doctors along the campaign route and so he had asked Dwight to close his office and accompany him for the duration of the presidential contest -- complete with the necessary portable laboratory equipment for him to run daily blood sugar determinations.

Dwight loved his life in Sarasota and he was not eager to leave his practice. The assignment would necessitate being away from his family for three months, also not a pleasant prospect. But he realized, as did his friends, that he might exert a great deal of influence over Silverbright and thereby help the anti-Communist cause. Beth agreed and so he had promised to accept the job if Warren won the presidential primaries.

Silverbright's primary campaign went smoothly, greased as it was by huge chunks of labor and foundation money. In West Virginia, where vote buying is a tradition, the money boys moved in and bought the county politicians. The day before the polls opened, the "slate" was distributed and the next day the hillbillies trooped to the polls and "voted" -- 5 dollars and one pint of whiskey richer. It was rumored that Silverbright's younger brother, Robbie, who was again his campaign manager, had run the payoff in West Virginia, but the press played it down. The rumor quickly died.

Again playing up the religious issue, Robbie said that the American people *had* to elect his brother Warren to prove that anti-Semitism was dead forever in the United States.

Robbie was young, arrogant, ruthless. He was hated and feared. He had to win, no matter what the contest -- or call the game off. And win he did. He captured the nomination for his brother. It took a great deal of lying, threatening and bribing; but Senator Warren Silverbright, a man with practically no experience in government and a poor Senate record (he was absent most of the time) captured the nomination for the presidency on a major party ticket.

As he had promised to do, Huckins departed immediately for Washington. Dwight had heard the rumors about the West Virginia payoff but he discounted them as the typical low-blow tactics of the opposition.

Silverbright's fight for the Presidency was all downhill. There had been some attempts by the opposition to expose Mrs. Silverbright's unconventional and immoral past. It was rumored that she had disappeared for prolonged periods of time at recent parties, but the press chose to ignore these stories and the people were given daily servings of Carla Silverbright on the front page: Carla coming out of church; Carla dedicating an orphanage; Carla baking a cake.

Presidential candidate Silverbright, under the careful tutelage of Carla, Robbie and Charlie Rubio promised the people everything in the book. Silverbright's nervous opponent promised everything too, but said that he would do it cheaper. The foundation money, part of America's pro-Communist "invisible government," kept pouring into the Silverbright campaign fund.

Very few knew where this money came from and no one asked -- no one but Dr. Huckins. Almost from the beginning, Dwight had become alarmed at the peculiar direction the campaign was taking. He tried to talk it over with Warren, but the Senator, as usual, was vague and facetious.

"Hell, Huck, you know how these elections are -- a lot of these ideas are just cooked up for election day. They're just cold potatoes on Wednesday morning."

Dwight, not satisfied with this explanation, sought out Robbie Silverbright in an attempt to effect some redirection of party strategy. After trying for days, Dwight finally caught up with Robbie at his Tulsa, Oklahoma, headquarters. The teletype was running and the Senator's brother, his hair falling over his boyish face, was giving orders to four frantic secretaries at once. Papers littered the room. The three telephones rang constantly.

"Mr. Silverbright, it's Governor Jameson." Robbie grabbed the phone from the secretary and, putting his feet up on the desk, said, "Hello, Jamie -- no, I wouldn't push the Cuban issue in your State. You're too close to Florida. Pound away on our demand that Russian troops be removed from Newfoundland -- a direct threat to Canadian and American security and all that. Yeah, that's right -- and push the religious issue -- *keep talking about the anti-Semitic revival.* Goodbye." He slammed down the phone, simultaneously turned to Dr. Huckins and winked broadly. "Don't change a winning system -- right, Huck ?" He did not offer a chair in spite of the superficial veneer of camaraderie. His eyes were cold and unfriendly.

"Robbie, what in blazes are you doing to this country?" Dwight almost shouted. "Do you think people are going to fall for this 26th parallel business? You can't give away American soil!"

What was known as The Silverbright Doctrine called for internationalizing the lower tip of Florida south of the 26th parallel. Florida was to be occupied by UN troops south of a line drawn between the town of Naples on the Gulf coast and Hollywood on the Atlantic coast -- this coincided with the 26th parallel. Senator Silverbright and vice-presidential candidate Gunther were barnstorming the country hammering away with this "honorable and peaceful solution to the Cuban crisis." This plan, they said, was considered a reasonable compromise with the demands of Dr. Brosnev, the President of Cuba. Brosnev had demanded that the whole of Florida be occupied by the UN to protect Cuba from forces hostile to its government. The Silverbright proposal fell far short of Cuba's demands, it was said, because the agreement would not only be restricted to the area south of the 26th parallel, but also carefully enumerated conditions to protect American security.

The main condition, one that the candidate boasted would raise the ire of the Cuban president, was that at all times the peace force must be comprised of at least 60% SEAPO troops (Southeastern Army Peace Organization), and under no circumstances were Cuban forces to be allowed to participate with the SEAPO force. They fully expected loud denunciations from Cuba, they said; but overall, it was felt that the plan would be workable and would "reduce tension." Robbie Silverbright also pointed out that the influx of military personnel would prove to be a boon to the sagging economy in the Miami area.

Robbie slammed his pencil down on the desk. "Huck, you and I have never agreed on how this campaign should be run..."

Dr. Huckins interrupted explosively, "It's not a question of the campaign, damn it, you're giving the Communists *American soil* -- have you gone crazy?"

Robbie leaped to his feet, his face flushed with anger. "Well, how the hell would you handle it? The area is hopelessly infiltrated with Cuban spies; riots and explosions have paralyzed Miami; the UN is yelling about discrimination against the damned Cubans -- what the hell would you do?"

Huckins ignored the outburst. "Where is all this big money coming from? You know Warren has no grass roots support."

For the first time Dwight noticed the four men sitting against the wall. They came over practically in formation. One of them spoke, "Mr. Silverbright, you have a meeting at 6:30."

"Yes," said Robbie, grabbing his hat and straightening his tie. "Huck, why don't you get out of this fight? I don't think you've got the stomach for it."

"This is no fight, Robbie, it's a sellout! You can tell Warren to get another doctor. I'm going back to Florida -- while there's still something left of it." He slammed the door behind him.

Blind with rage, he walked through the hotel lobby. A woman reporter caught him by the arm. "Aren't you Dr. Huckins, advisor to Senator Silverbright?"

"No, madam, I am not. I have just resigned."

"Oh, my," she exclaimed. "Are you going to make a public announcement?" She fumbled for a pencil and pad.

"No, I'm not announcing anything -- you just got yourself an exclusive!"

Nothing could stop the Silverbright juggernaut. Warren Silverbright became the first presidential candidate ever to carry every State in the Union but one. Florida, alone, dismembered, strife-torn and embittered, abstained from the election.

6. Seneca

R.A. Seneca was born in Tuna, Russia. His real name was Yuni Rudenko. His parents were village farmers and they, like their ancestors, would live and die in the vast area of Mongol Russia, without ever seeing the sea. Moscow would be almost as foreign to them as New York. Their son was bright, but quickly came under the influence of an evil force that was as strange to them as the Indian Ocean -- messianic Communism. The parents were, of course, communized, but they were not Communists. They worshipped, secretly, as did their fathers. They worked hard and believed in just recompense for that work. They did not believe in sharing the product of their labor with the indolent; they knew that it bred further indolence. They endured the yoke of tyranny silently, grimly and with Christian faith that Russian tyranny would be overthrown as predicted by Our Lady of Fatima in 1917. They knew well the story of the Miracle of the Sun and how seventy thousand people, on October 13, 1917, had watched the Portugese sky as the sun spun around three times and dived toward the earth. At that time the Mother of God spoke to three children and said: "In the end, my Immaculate Heart will triumph. The Holy Father will consecrate Russia to me, which will be converted and a time of peace will be granted to humanity."

That the miracle had happened was true beyond doubt. Russia would be converted. The Rudenkos were convinced that it would happen in their generation.

As their son developed the coldness of eye and cruelty of mouth that is typical of Communist youth, they knew instinctively that they could not speak to him of such things. The messianism of Yuni Rudenko's younger days changed inexorably into the cynical, cold cruelty of a Communist on top of his local heap -- a heap of corpses, near-corpses and terrified peasants.

Yuni Rudenko, alias Seneca, had the large, blunt and humorless face of a Russian peasant. His would have been the undistinguished face of the masses were it not for one distinctive characteristic, and it was not a pretty one: a deep, round scar below the left eye from a bullet wound. The scar tugged at the lower lid giving him the perpetual appearance of a man about to cry --but only on one side of his face. The other side was frozen peasant, completely unaware of the sadness of its neighbor. This startling dichotomy of visage coupled with the largeness of his head gave one the impression of looking at a man with two heads. This was a person once seen always remembered --with revulsion.

At 16 Yuni was already important in the local village apparatus. As his power grew, his arrogance and viciousness grew with it. As with other intelligent young Communists, Yuni quickly learned that the theories of Communism and its save-the-world messianism were sucker bait for stupid, self-certified "intellectuals" everywhere. These pseudo-intellectuals were, in effect, the tools used by all the realistic Communist elite throughout the world. Individually such dupes were about as important as a drop of oil; collectively, they oiled the skids for the Russian advance. Eventually, and without exception in every country, the intellectuals' own blood became the final lubricant.

Yuni revelled in goading his tight-lipped father. "Tell me, Father," he said one evening across the dinner table, "where is the soul located? My anatomy teacher says it's most likely in the gizzard. But I don't suppose that you agree." He studied his father's wrinkled face, expecting his usual taciturnity. His mother continued to eat her soup, but she was not tasting it. She was praying that her husband would be able to continue to absorb the shock of their son's abusive attacks, although she knew that he was nearing the breaking point. Yuni broke off a piece of black bread and wagged it at his father. "Perhaps, Father, you could come to school with me tomorrow. We could operate on me and take out my gizzard and you could show us the soul."

The father laid his spoon carefully on the table. "My son," he said, looking up for the first time, "if the gizzard contains the soul, then I am certain that your gizzard would not reveal one." The boy turned livid as he glared at his father. His mother's mouth fell open. She dared not breathe. Yuri slammed his spoon into his soup bowl, causing soup to fly in every direction. He jumped to his feet, overturning his chair, and bolted from the room. Mrs. Rudenko buried her face in her hands. Her husband stared sightlessly across the table.

The next day Yuri went to the local party headquarters and denounced his family as hoarders. Yuri stood on the other side of the road and watched the police enter his family's simple cottage. They immediately reappeared dragging Mrs. Rudenko by one leg across the rough gravel. Her screams of pain elicited peals of laughter from the uniformed men. As the old man reached down to pick up his wife by the shoulders, a rifle butt smashed into the rear of his skull. Yuri's face, heretofore expressionless, contorted into a one-sided grin.

As the truck containing his groaning and battered parents pulled away, Yuri, with a flick of his head, motioned to two young men standing in the shade of a nearby tree. Each held a pail of gasoline. They quickly advanced and flung the gasoline through the cottage door. Yuri, with deliberate slowness and obvious relish, strolled to the front door, lit a match and tossed it in. His two henchmen watched in awe as he casually walked away, never looking back at the flaming inferno that had been his home.

Yuri was sent to the NKVD spy school where he was taught Greek, English and all the crafts of espionage and assassination techniques. From there he was sent to managerial school to get a proper cover for his future operations. Soon thereafter, under the name of R.A. Seneca, he appeared in Greece where he set up a small shoe factory. Next he took out Greek citizenship papers. From then on his rise in the Communist apparatus was meteoric and he was soon ready for transfer to the United States. By the time Warren Silverbright was elected to the Presidency, R.A. Seneca was already in Washington -- "a highly respected Greek citizen" attached to the United Nations Area Affairs Committee. He was almost immediately assigned to President Silverbright as "UN Assistant to the President, Area Four." Silverbright facetiously referred to him as his "unemployed shoe salesman." But the relationship was not a happy one for the President. He could hardly act, it seemed, without Seneca's approval. The Executive branch had wrested total power from the Legislative branch which had become nothing more than a debating society. This power had then been diffused into the UN and the President realized, vaguely, that his job was not what he had expected.

One of Seneca's first jobs as UN Assistant to the President was to wire for Dr. Dwight

Huckins in Sarasota. Although Seneca had recommended a psychiatrist from the UN staff to be Silverbright's personal physician, the President had insisted on having Huckins. A week after President Silverbright was elected in November of 1976, Dwight received the telegram from Washington:

> The White House, Washington, D.C. -- It is with the greatest pleasure that I inform you of your appointment as personal physician to President Silverbright. This appointment is subject to the approval of the United Nations Area Affairs Committee and, of course, your willingness to accept. Cordially yours, R.A. Seneca, Deputy United Nations Assistant to the President, Area Four.

This Area Four business irritated Huckins immensely. "U.S. Government" was disappearing from all official communications. UN-A4 was even appearing on the new dollar bills. Once during his days as a Senator, when Silverbright had been in Huckins' office for his regular checkup, Dwight had expressed alarm about the UN-A4 propaganda flooding the country but Warren had been unimpressed. "They're just a little overzealous, Huck," he had said. "After all, they did depose Castro and they did move those Russian troops out of Newfoundland. I think we have made real progress toward a lasting peace through the United Nations but we can't accomplish everything overnight."

Dwight had always hated this patronizing tone of Silverbright's because he knew that

Silverbright read very little and seldom troubled himself with affairs of state other than those concerning his immediate political future. When still a member of the Senate, Warren had been ignorant of the subversive forces playing around him. But he was also ignorant of his ignorance and thought he could cast a proper vote in the Senate simply by using common sense -- of which he had very little -- but he was ignorant of *that*, too.

Earlier, during the months when the Russian degenerate and murderer Prusakova and his Chinese accomplices had been carving up South America, Silverbright was chuckling about the "Sino-Soviet split." And later, even when the Chinese took over El Paso, Senator Silverbright had remained undisturbed.

Now, Dwight recognized the President's summons, by way of Seneca, as an appeal for help. Obviously Warren Silverbright was in deep trouble and so, therefore, was the country. Someone had to counterbalance the UN, the labor racketeers, the invisible government of wealthy power-seekers who utilized both of these -- and the ubiquitous Communists who actually controlled them all. The President's fanatical younger brother, Robbie, was a separate menace all by himself.

Silverbright had no one to whom he could turn. Dwight dreaded Washington, the uprooting of his family, the political intrigues. He especially dreaded dealing with the arrogant UN officials who had usurped enough power to make the United States little more than a province of a United Nations dictatorship. But he also knew that President Warren Silverbright was entirely unequipped to deal with these crafty men, and would be their captive if there was no countervailing influence. If he were at the President's side, at least someone there would be representing the best interests of the United States.

Dwight decided to go back to Washington. He accepted the appointment and became thereby the unofficial presidential advisor as well as White House physician.

7. The Trusting Place

Beth Huckins stared out of the kitchen window of their home in the Georgetown section of Washington. After the lush green of Florida it was difficult to adjust again to the somberness of Washington winters. The barrenness of the trees, especially in late afternoon, Particularly depressed her. It was always a relief to see Dwight pulling into the driveway or the children careening toward the house on their bicycles.

"Beth, I'm home," Dwight yelled, as he closed the front door. She always saw him coming, making his daily announcement unnecessary. But she never told him because the greeting filled her with warmth and heralded the beginning of the part of the day that really mattered.

Dwight took off his shoes and put his feet up on the coffee table. Beth curled up beside him. They sipped a highball and reviewed the events of the day. "Did you see Wallis Westphall's column this morning?" Beth asked.

"No, why?" Dwight lit a cigar and tossed the match in the ashtray.

"Well, you know what a gossip he is. He says that some important government official's wife is seeing a certain Polish diplomat..."

"Beth," Dwight interrupted, "you know how unreliable Westphall is." He felt a vague foreboding and uneasiness. Carla, he feared, was continuing her immoral behavior even as the President's wife. He had no proof and, because of his relationship to the President, knew that she would bend every effort to keep it from him.

"Dwight, you know I'm not a gossip but I was wondering ... about Carla. Do you suppose..."

Dwight tapped his cigar against the ashtray. "Sweetheart, I don't know. I don't even like to think about it. Half the people in Washington are compromised one way or another. Think what could happen if the right people discovered that the President's wife..."

The back door slammed and David entered whistling and swinging a fielder's mit. "Hi, Dad -- when do we eat, Mom?" They greeted him warmly, glad at the opportunity to drop the unpleasant subject.

"Wash your face and call your sister," Beth said, "I'll put dinner on the table." She tugged Dwight by the hand. "Finish your drink in the kitchen?"

In another part of town, at the very same time, another couple was discussing the Westphall article.

"Forget it, darling. You know what an imbecile Westphall is and, besides, I'm not the only man in the Polish Legation." Carla dropped two frosty ice cubes into a highball glass and did not reply.

Vladimir Jasinski Looked like a giant blonde hawk. He had a massive nose and a prominent pointed chin. His dark brown eyes made a startling contrast with his big, bushy blonde eyebrows and thick, unruly blonde hair. He had a maleness about him that captivated the opposite sex. At Embassy functions he would wear his Polish officers uniform with the red and gold epaulettes and generally dominate the gathering -- somewhat to the chagrin of the Polish Ambassador.

Jasinski had a hold on Carla that none of her other lovers had had. He made her jealous as no other man had ever been able to do. Their trysting place was a small, fashionable apartment near the Senate Office Building. She would elude her Secret Service guards and enter the apartment through a back entrance.

Carla poured a jigger of Scotch over the ice. Vladimir, who was that woman in the picture with you in yesterday's papers ?" Her green eyes studied him intently from across the room as she waited for his answer.

Jasinski casually rose from the couch and turned on the phonograph. "I think she's a reporter for the WASHINGTON EAGLE. The Ambassador took a fancy to her and insisted that she stay for lunch."

"I can see why he took an interest in her and I'm surprised that you didn't -- or did you?"

"No," he laughed, "she was a bore, really -- are you going to give me that drink or do I have to do some sort of obeisance for it?" He smiled down at her, took her chin between his fingers and artfully deflected her suspicions.

"Yes," she said as her respirations deepened and her face flushed. "You'll have to do obeisance -- the kind you always do so well." She handed him his drink and pressed herself against him. That familiar glaze to her eyes told him she was already gripped with a flood of passion. Carla pulled out his shirt in back, ran her hands below his belt and pulled him firmly against her. As they kissed she felt him swell with passion. She took his glass and put it on the table. "Drink that later, darling. It's been a long time --I've thought about this all day and I couldn't sleep last night."

Jasinski carried her heaving little body into the brightly lit bedroom. Carla had it arranged like a television studio with glaring light cascading off the brilliant white sheets and through the large mirrors she had placed on both sides of the bed. The apposed mirrors, reflecting each others' image, gave the impression of a hundred beds juxtaposed in each direction. Like a music lover with his woofers and tweeters, Carla had to envelope sex and be completely enveloped by it.

"Hurry, hurry!" she pleaded. Carla tore at his shirt as he placed her on the drum-tight sheet. Vladimir Jasinski gave Carla the only kind of peace and happiness she ever knew or understood or cared about. She worshipped Priapus and knew no other god.

* * *

Eighteen months of seeing the nation's problems from the inside passed quickly for the Huckins family. The children were in private school with the children of other government notables and doing very well. Beth had adjusted to their new life and was keeping a diary for future publication, but Dwight was bored with the lack of medical work to be done. After 10 years of general practice, it was hard to get used to the absence of any real medical challenge, except for the President's diabetes. An occasional dripping nose of some department head's child, an anxiety attack in a White House secretary --these were hardly medicine as he had known

it. He wondered, uncomfortably, if he would lose his touch when this was all over. But there was little time for such musings. President Silverbright respected Dr. Huckins deeply and insisted that he be party to all decisions, despite the grumblings from Seneca and the Cabinet. Silverbright would even sign papers without reading them if Huckins' initials, denoting approval, were on them.

One of the prerogatives of Dwight's position was a chauffeured limousine and this he always took advantage of on Mondays. Although he was opposed to bureaucratic waste of taxpayers' money, he felt that this one weekly round-trip from home to office and back was justified because he utilized the time in the car to read the newspapers and catch up on his medical journals.

Halfway across town late one Monday afternoon he unfolded the WASHINGTON EVENING HERALD and was electrified by the two-inch headline:

PRESIDENT AGREES
U.N. NEUTRALIZATION
BROWNSVILLE AREA

Dwight read on, unbelieving:

United Nations International News Service, May 12, 1978 --

The historic Silverbright Doctrine is back in the news today as Brownsville, Texas, is declared a neutral zone. In a joint communique issued by UN Area 4, Deputy Assistant R.A. Seneca and President Warren Silverbright, it was stated that Brownsville, Texas, which is just below the 26th parallel, would be turned over to the peace-keeping forces as an additional peace buffer zone.

Large troop concentrations in Matamoros, Mexico, across the border from

Brownsville, have been reported recently. Chairman Ivan Prusakova of the USSR had claimed that Naval Air Forces in Brownsville were a threat to Mexican security and that the Russian troops in Matamoros were there to defend Mexico's border from aggression "if necessary."

A communique from Moscow stated that Mr. Prusakova lauds the further extension of the Silverbright Doctrine as a giant step toward lasting peace. He cited the occupation of El Paso, Texas, 8 years ago by SWAPO forces~ as establishing a precedent for the latest move. El Paso is well above the 26th parallel, but also on the Mexican border.

SWAPO spokesman Samuel Yen stated today that this tiny area in the remote southeast corner of Texas is not considered strategically important. With the neutralization of Ukinawa and Guam last year, he added, Brownsville remained the last unneutralized area below the 26th parallel except Hawaii and was, consequently, one of the few remaining areas of disagreement with Chairman Prusakova.

In an unprecedented move, the Nobel Peace Prize Committee has announced a "Decade Peace Prize" to be presented jointly to Chairman Prusakova and President Silverbright. This is an entirely new award, a committee spokesman said. It is called the "Decade Peace Prize" to point up the immense contribution toward peace in this decade made by USSR Chairman Prusakova and the President of the United States.

Dwight immediately ordered his driver to turn around and drive back to the White House. How had all this happened without his knowing

-- and right under his nose! Brownsville was vital to the protection of the Gulf Coast of the United States. Its neutralization, Dwight realized, would immediately lay the American government open to Communist demands on Corpus Christi and its vital Naval installations only a few hundred miles farther north of the Gulf Coast. The President knew this. He had often discussed it with Dwight. Huckins felt a deep sense of rage and betrayal.

The limousine pulled up in front of the White House and Dwight was out of the car before it could come to a full stop. His anger mounted as he strode briskly up the front stairs, ignoring the Marine guard who saluted him smartly.

Dwight burst into the President's private dining room. "Silver, what in hell are you up to ?" His tie was a little askew; his respiration fast. Carla looked at Dwight quizzically.

"What on earth is the matter, Huck?" Not waiting for his answer, she added: "You look as if the market had just crashed. For heaven's sake, darling, have a drink and gather yourself." She came forward and pecked him on the check.

"Carla," the President said in an unusually abrupt manner, "I know why Dwight is here and I think you had better leave us alone for a moment." He had never spoken to his wife like this before. Carla was accustomed to being privy to all his secrets and was hurt by the sudden exclusion.

"Very well," she said with careful indifference, "I'll be in the bedroom." The rapid pace of her steps revealed the annoyance she felt.

The two men looked at each other. Dwight waited.

"You think I am a fool, don't you?" the President finally said. His eyes dropped to the floor. For the first time in his life, Warren Silverbright looked older than he was. His hand shook, as he sipped his coffee.

Dwight stared at the broken man. The silence in the room was almost audible. "Silver," he hesitated. "What am I to think when you agree to such a disastrous thing?" Dwight put his hand on the President's shoulder. "For God's sake, tell me what happened."

"It was that damned Seneca, Dwight. He blackmailed me into it and after I agreed and it was announced, I realized it wasn't worth it -- not even for Carla."

"Carla! What the hell has she got to do with it?"

The President looked at Dwight, his face ashen. "Do you remember the old stories the opposition used to peddle, especially during the campaign, about Carla and the exPresident? Well, Seneca and his crowd have photographs. They showed them to me and they show *everything*. I mean they show Carla..." Warren could not finish. He got up from the table and moved to where Dwight had slumped into a chair. "Then they said they had other pictures of Carla taken since I became President. I refused to look at them. I just wanted to agree to anything -- and get rid of them." He wiped his sweating brow with a shaking hand. "Dwight, I haven't eaten all day. I took 40 units of insulin this morning and I think I'm going into shock." He clutched Dwight's chair to steady himself.

Dwight, suddenly reminded of his professional responsibility, jumped to his feet and eased the President into his chair. Warren's eyes were rolling back and his skin was cold and clammy. Huckins dashed into the adjoining room and returned with his emergency bag. He took out a vial of concentrated glucose, a tourniquet and a syringe. Working quickly, calmly and methodically, he applied the tourniquet at the upper arm, found a large vein and shot the glucose in as rapidly as he could. The President's eyes flickered. He sighed deeply and lifted his head. "What happened, Dwight? Did I have another one?"

"Yes, but you're O.K. now. Go back to the table and eat your dinner whether you want it or not." Not looking up, he gathered his medical equipment together.

The President looked at him imploringly and the questions tumbled out. "What am I going to do, Huck? Shall we fortify Corpus Christi?" Dwight placed his equipment carefully in his bag and did not answer. "You won't mention about Carla to anyone, will you, Huck?"

"Of course, I won't mention Carla," Dwight replied irritably, "I'm your doctor -- remember?"

"Yes, and you're the only person I can trust."

Huckins avoided his gaze. "I'll check with you in an hour. Don't take insulin until I get a blood sugar report in the morning." He clamped the bag shut and left, dejected and disgusted.

The President continued staring at the door long after Dwight had closed it. The Washington Monument, visible through the open window, was a foggy white streak in the darkness. The peculiar sound of soundlessness had returned to the room. It was broken only by the sobs of the President of the United States...

8. The Cabinet Meeting

Warren Silverbright was not a man without conscience. The deep searing pain caused by the discovery of Carla's infidelities had changed him. His facetiousness, his hedonistic attitude toward life and his sophomoric approach to serious problems were gone. Everyone, including those who had been manipulating him, recognized the dramatic change in the President. The conspirators realized, to their chagrin, that Carla's exposure had had an effect on the President opposite from that intended.

Warren never mentioned the pictures to Carla. He would not, in fact, could not, stop loving her, no matter what she did. He couldn't change that, but he couldn't change the pictures either -- the hurt was always with him. Silverbright had become stubborn and recalcitrant at meetings, disagreeing with and disapproving of almost anything proposed by either Seneca or Vice President Gunther. This was not so much from any new understanding of the gigantic plot around him as it was from frustration and a blind attempt to strike back at things he could not entirely comprehend.

Even brother Robbie was not immune from Warren's wild and irrational attacks. When Robbie suggested that Dr. Huckins be replaced, the President flew into a rage. Two days later he ordered Robbie on an extended "good-will tour" of the Far East and personally handed him his diplomatic papers.

Robbie leaned across the President's desk, his face contorted with rage. "You can't shove me aside after all I've done for you, Warren -- you're going to regret this."

Warren leaped to his feet and leaned across the desk. Their faces almost touched. "Are you threatening me, Mr. Attorney General -- are you threatening the President of the United States?"

Robbie's eyes narrowed and his answer came out in a hiss, "Yes, you silly fool --yes, I am!" He wheeled, clutching his papers, and stalked from the room.

* * *

The first Cabinet meeting since the black-mail episode, three weeks previously, was to begin at 9 A.M. Its members, with Robbie conspicuously absent, sat around the long, highly polished, glass-topped table, awaiting the arrival of the President. The Secretaries of

Defense, State, Treasury, Public Information and Interior were present. But the gathering looked more like a United Nations meeting than a traditional Presidential Cabinet session. Along with the department heads, sat the ubiquitous Seneca, Vice President Gunther -- placed as usual to Seneca's right -- and at the far end of the table was the taciturn, gray eminence of General Jawaral Rangadoo of the Indian Third Army, now commanding SWAPO, the UN's Southwest Army Peace Organization. He had taken command following General Swindler's death. The General had been killed instantly when his car was dynamited in El Paso, Texas. The bombing was reported by the press as an anti-UN maneuver by diehard Texans." The Texas underground apprehended the assassin, who turned out to be a member of the Civil Liberties League, a Communist and UN-front organization. The agent provocateur, the most effective weapon in the Communist arsenal for dividing a nation against itself, had accomplished two objectives with the murder of Swindler. He had given the Texas underground the label of "warmongering fanatics" and, at the same time, had propelled the hard-core Communist, Rangadoo, into Command of SWAPO.

Interspersed among the department heads sat other UN officials. They talked vociferously to each other in foreign languages and ignored the uncomprehending Cabinet members. The Americans looked out of place and vaguely uncomfortable.

The President and Dr. Huckins entered. Silence fell over the room and the Cabinet members shuffled to their feet. "Good morning, Mr. President," they said in unison. The UN officials, their faces suddenly expressionless, did not rise.

President Silverbright opened the leather-bound folder before him. "The first item on the agenda," the President began monotonously, "concerns the sudden rise in the consumer price index..."

The meeting went routinely enough at first but the President became more irritable as it progressed. The UN people kept their silence and appeared completely unperturbed by the frequent acid comments directed toward them by Silverbright.

"The South Africa situation appears to be unchanged this week," the President said. "The South Africans have now held the UN Army at bay for six years. The Indian Gurka troops now being used against them have been totally ineffective, General Rangadoo." He scowled down the long table at the General. "Would you care to comment on this, General?" The General did not answer.

The Secretary of Agriculture nervously attempted to change the subject. "Mr. President, the wheat surplus this fiscal year..."

"Shut up, Wilson," the President snapped. "General Rangadoo hasn't answered my question." The President glared at the General who remained immobile.

Seneca spoke for the first time. His weeping left eye appeared even more bloodshot than usual and the hole below it darker than ever. "Mr. President, perhaps if we increased the UN appropriation, as I have suggested. .

"No!" Silverbright slammed his fist down with such force that it shattered the glass table top. He turned pale as excruciating pain paralyzed his right hand. Dwight realized that the President had almost certainly fractured his wrist and rushed to assist him. Silverbright, holding his injured wrist, got to his feet uncertainly. Halfway to the door he turned and pointed a trembling finger toward the other end of the room. His voice was strident and quivering. "And ... and I want that damn UN flag out of here next week. This is supposed to be a *Cabinet meeting* -- not an international club!" Nauseated with pain, he reeled from the room leaning on Dwight's shoulder.

The thunderstruck Cabinet members, not knowing quite what to do with themselves, shifted in their seats, cleared their throats and glanced nervously at Seneca. The UN officials sat in stony silence.

President Warren Silverbright's usefulness to the Communist conspiracy was definitely at an end.

9. The Assassination

Huckins' office adjoined the President's and from certain angles, the President's desk could be seen through the doctor's office door. It was Dwight's custom to leave early on Friday afternoons and go to Chesapeake Bay with Beth and the children for the weekend. He always left by the rear door of his office and always notified the President's secretary, Communications and Bethesda Naval Hospital when he went so that Captain Greene, a Naval Medical officer and an old friend from his Navy days, would be alerted to stand by in his absence. The time of his departure every weekend was known by dozens of people. Huckins would often wonder later why he hadn't realized the importance of that and also of the fact that during the period from about three in the afternoon until five, the President was usually alone -- unless some world crisis was disrupting the routine. He would later remember how the President had often mentioned jokingly that people didn't seem to care whether

or not there was a president from three o'clock
Friday afternoon until Monday morning.

It was the weekend of the Fourth of July,
1978, and the White House had even fewer occupants than it usually had on Friday afternoons.
President Silverbright, his right arm in a plaster
cast, was talking to one of his writers on the telephone about an address he was to give the next
day. The doctor made his usual check-out calls,
waved to the President from his door without
disturbing his conversation and went out
through his private entrance.

"Silver looks terrible," the doctor reflected
as he descended the stairs to the door that led
out onto the White House lawn. "He never
should have left the Senate -- and he knows it."
As he opened the door to the lawn, the blast of
hot summer air reminded him: the keys to the
boat. "Damn it, they're in my desk." He
slammed the half-opened door shut and ran up
the stairs two at a time. He had left the door to
the President's office half closed. As he started
into his office, he heard someone speaking in the
next room. It was Seneca's voice. Seneca was
supposed to be in Los Angeles. What was he doing here? From across the room through the
crack on the hinged side of the door, Dwight
could glimpse the President seated at his desk.
Not knowing quite why, Huckins froze, his hand
still gripping the doorknob and his eyes riveted
on the President.

"Mr. President, your lines of communica-
tion from this office are temporarily out of or-

der," Seneca's voice hinted of arrogance -- and something more. "Take your pen and write what I say," he demanded.

"What in hell are you up to, Seneca?" The President's voice was tinged with fear.

"Write the words 'chest pain' -- quickly!" Huckins could see the President's head bend over his pen as he began to write. With sudden realization, Dwight snapped to life and was half-way across his office when there was an explosion like the discharge of a cap pistol. The President's head thumped against his desktop. A door banged closed.

Immediately Huckins was assailed by a familiar and terrifying smell -- bitter almonds -- cyanide! With the smell of bitter almonds at his nostrils, his own death was only a short breath away. A reflex born of experience with dangerous chemicals propelled him down the back stairs and out to the lawn. The President had become the victim of a classic Communist weapon of assassination, the cyanide gas gun.

Dwight had to get away from there and quickly. Numb with shock, he started to run for his car, but realizing that this would attract attention, he slowed to a brisk walk. His head was bursting with pain and he felt a slight nausea.

Sitting in his car with the engine idling, he tried to collect his thoughts from the welter of confusion and terror that gripped him. Something had to be done immediately, but what? If only the throbbing in his head would stop! The trip to Chesapeake Bay would have to be cancelled -- no, that would look as though he knew something. Who would believe his incredible story? He had to have time to think. They would call it a heart attack, which was routine Communist technique in cyanide murders, but Carla at least had to know the truth. As family physician to the President, it was certainly his duty to break the news to her in spite of his contempt for her. Dwight felt obligated to find Carla before the murder became public knowledge.

Picking up the telephone in his car, he identified himself and asked the operator to locate Mrs. Silverbright. He drove slowly down Pennsylvania Avenue toward the Capitol aware of no particular destination, but feeling the need to keep moving. The operator still did not call back. Surely Carla was not on one of her escapades at this, of all times --she might not be located for hours!

He turned the radio on and not really hearing the recorded music, prayed that the body of the President would not be found until he located Carla. The music stopped abruptly. Dwight held his breath. "Here is a late bulletin from the WUNO newsroom: Fresh border clashes have erupted at the 26th parallel, a few miles west of Hollywood, Florida. UN forces in the neutralized zone were apparently ambushed by units of the so-called MacArthur Legion. One Congolese officer was killed. No other casualties have been reported. Stay tuned for the complete news at..." Dwight snapped off the radio and picked up the buzzing telephone. "Huckins here -- hello, Carla? Where are you?" He tried to keep the urgency out of his voice. "Can you meet me at the Lincoln Memorial in ten minutes? Good." Dwight's tires screeched as he made a U-turn and sped down Pennsylvania Avenue.

"And Carla was going to 'handle' the Communists," he thought, "she and that smartaleck brother Robbie." He dreaded facing Carla. Polygamous as she was, she was very dependent on and fond of Warren Silverbright -- in her own peculiar way. He would be glad when this grim chore was done. His obligation to Carla would then be discharged and he would never have to see her again. He wished he had never come to Washington --what good had he done? It would have been better, he mused, to have stayed in Sarasota and helped his friend, Tom Mahan, with the underground movement.

When Dwight reached the Lincoln Memorial he was surprised and relieved to see that Carla had arrived before him. She was standing on the Memorial steps wearing a green cotton dress and looking cool and fresh despite the shimmering July heat. "Hello, Lover," she greeted him gaily. "You know, I've decided those gray temples are just the thing for you. Of course, you don't really need them as much as Warren, but they're appealing nonetheless." He started to speak, but she continued. "Why the urgent meeting, Dwight? Have you decided you can't resist me any longer and if so, couldn't you pick a more private place?" She smiled up at him.

When breaking news of death, Dwight had learned from long experience to come to the point at once. "Carla -- I've got dreadful news. Warren has been assassinated."

"That's ridiculous," she said. Her mouth began to move as if to explain. Her mind had registered something that was not possible and as Dwight watched, the life seemed to drain from her face, changing her alabaster skin to gray. The words would not come.

Abraham Lincoln, towering above them, seemed also to grieve -- not for President Silverbright, but for a collapsing America.

10. The Execution

As Huckins had predicted, the President's death was called a heart attack, his quickly scribbled note being held as consummate proof of that diagnosis. The telephone had been out of order, fatefully, at the hour of his attack and he had, it was said, scribbled the note so that the world would know. "A brilliant mind thinking right up to the last" the NEW TIMES editorialized. The controlled press wailed about how the "rightwingers" and "super-patriots" had driven the young President to an early grave. The "burden of hate," especially the acrimonious criticism of the Silverbright Doctrine, had been "more than his broad shoulders could bear." It was nothing less than assassination by slander, they said, and some papers suggested that henceforth criticism of the President be considered seditious.

Backing up the Communist-dominated press, many ministers screeched from their pulpits that Christ had left the hearts of the people.

"This crime must not go unpunished," they sermonized. "The hate-mongers must receive their retribution -- 'Vengeance is mine; I will repay, saith the Lord.' "

Those ministers who did not agree with these vicious and hysterical outbursts dared not speak. Dissidence meant immediate expulsion from the Federal Conference of Churches, withdrawal of federal funds and sudden death to the minister's church.

Dwight had kept silent about witnessing the assassination. Immediately after his meeting with Carla, he made contact with an underground agent and through him, consulted with Tom Mahan, head of the secret MacArthur Legion headquartered in Sarasota, Florida. Mahan advised him to keep silent because no one would believe the incredible truth even if the papers revealed it, and they probably would not. Washington law enforcement was by now so corrupt, and Communist infiltration so complete in the upper echelons of the Federal Government that if Dwight revealed what he knew, the Communists would surely destroy him, possibly even by accusing him of the crime.

Dwight remained silent but the hysteria reached such alarming proportions that Mahan finally agreed the facts must somehow be revealed. No outspoken anti-Communist was safe. High school and college students were running wild. A college professor who had attacked the 26th parallel agreement was severely beaten; A Conservative student at Georgetown University was strangled to death by irate young radicals; Senator Mad-don, an outspoken anti-Communist, was shot by a "Cuban refugee" and narrowly escaped death.

Tom Mahan released the true facts of the assassination to trusted underground friends on a Monday. By Wednesday a crudely mimeographed sheet was flooding the streets of every major city in the United States. It gave the exact time of the assassination, the method used and it accused "high officials" of the murder. Because of his airtight alibi, Seneca's name was withheld. To have revealed it, under the circumstances, would have only discredited the entire counter-cybernetic operation. Seneca's trip to Los Angeles had been carefully publicized, in retrospect, for obvious reasons.

Dwight waited with a sense of uneasiness for the frantic denials and screams of pain from the Communists and their lick-spittles in the American press. What would they do? They would know from the detailed information given in the underground's printed exposé that someone had witnessed the crime. Dwight's alibi was sound. He had checked out before the murder with a half-dozen different people. But was it sound enough? He could have come back, as of course he had. That no one had seen him was a calculated risk he had to take. Otherwise, the mass psychosis gripping the nation might break the back of the anti-Communist movement as the people looked for a scapegoat.

As the days passed, Dr. Huckins' uneasiness increased. Seneca's alibi was far better than his, and Dwight was well aware of the conspiracy's thoroughness when it came to the assassination of important people. A second and even third victim were always kept in reserve to be thrown into the breech and blamed for the murder if the first accusation proved unsuccessful. Obviously the anti-Communist movement was not going to wither away under the intensive propaganda barrage being directed its way; for the circular from the MacArthur Legion had served its purpose well and the national hysteria was dying down. Whom would they use as their scapegoat now?

Six days had passed and the press was still strangely silent. Dwight sensed that something big was about to break. On Saturday morning he sat down to breakfast in his Georgetown home. Neither he nor any member of the family had ventured from Georgetown since the day after the assassination. All non-military officials had been ordered to stay out of Washington for security reasons. The city was completely chaotic and unsafe. As he was putting his coffee cup to his lips, Beth entered, pale and trembling. "What's the matter?" he asked, putting down the cup.

"Oh, God, Dwight -- look at the headlines." She plopped the BALTIMORE POST in front of him and began to cry. The headline hit Dwight like a blow to the stomach: "President's Widow Indicted For Murder." He quickly skimmed the article, breakfast forgotten.

Washington (UN-A4 News Service) July 10, 1978 -- A cleaning woman, who reportedly narrowly escaped death, stated late last night that she witnessed the cold-blooded murder of President Warren Silverbright. The woman, Mrs. Ella Stubbins, 58, of 4700 B Street, S.E., has pointed the finger of guilt at the late President's widow, Mrs. Carla Silverbright. Her story has electrified the world and promises to reveal the most sensational murder story of the century. "I was cleaning the office of Doctor Huckins -- he's the President's doctor. Mrs. Silverbright entered the President's office and killed her husband with some sort of gas instrument." The maid further related that she herself barely escaped death from the fumes by running through a back entrance.

The Armed Forces Institute of Pathology has announced that blood and tissue studies of the late President have been completed and they confirm Mrs. Stubbins' story. The Institute report reveals that cyanide gas, a deadly and instantaneous poison was used to murder the President. Apparently a gas pistol which ejects a spray of the deadly substance was used for the crime. An intensive search for the murder weapon is being conducted, Washington police have announced.

The press took up the new heading without a miss in cues and the new victim was thrown into the breech:

Supreme Court Justice Douglas Whitehead, in an interview today, said that Mrs. Silverbright was undoubtedly an agent of the so-called MacArthur Legion Underground group. Other speculations have centered around Mrs. Silverbright's social life. The Attorney General and brother of the late President, Robert Silverbright, stated late this morning that a close friend of the widow's had revealed more damaging evidence against Mrs. Silverbright. "The whole thing is a pretty rotten picture," he added.

"So that's it," Dwight said aloud. "That slimy little snake Robbie is in on a frame-up of Carla -- his own sister-in-law!" For the first time he realized that Beth was crying uncontrollably. He took her in his arms.

"Dwight, what are we going to do? Carla did some bad things, but does she deserve this?" Dwight held her and did not answer.

Tom Mahan communicated with Dwight immediately through underground intermediaries. He anticipated, correctly, that Dwight would feel obligated to come to Carla's defense because of her non-complicity in the murder. Mahan knew there had been some animosity between the two but he also knew Dwight Huckins and his strong sense of fair play. He urged Dwight not to expose himself. Carla's plight was obviously hopeless, he explained, largely of her own making, and by jeopardizing himself and his family, Dwight would accomplish nothing. Dwight agreed to remain silent although the decision rankled. His dislike for Carla had lately metamorphosed into disgust, but to see her die for the crime perpetrated by the hideous and evil Seneca was almost unbearable. However, Huckins had actually realized that Carla was doomed when he read Saturday morning's headline.

Justice Whitehead was appointed to lead the Board of Investigation and R.A. Seneca was appointed to the Board by former Vice-President Gunther the day after Gunther was sworn in as the new President of the United States.

Carla with her strong instinct for self-preservation, fought like a tigress. She was confident that Jasinski would verify that she had been with him at the time of the murder. But at the trial he only implicated her further. She then said that the cleaning woman, who had made the original accusation against her, was a Soviet agent. She was right, of course, but how could she prove it? About once a week she would change attorneys because, she said, they were all against her. She was only partially right -- no attorney would have the courage to delve into the facts behind this case: not when it was so obvious that very important and ruthless people expected her conviction. The slightest bit of prying might uncover some very sensitive nerve endings, for Carla had covered a lot of ground in Washington and one never knew, under the circumstances, when a photograph might appear. One such mistake could not only ruin a lawyer's career but it could be decidedly unhealthy physically for him and for his family.

In desperation, Carla called Dwight and asked him to visit her at the Federal Penitentiary. He, of course, agreed to come -- no one else had; none of the myriad of lovers, none of the politicians -- no one. To visit her would stain one with suspicion. The columnists had raised the question of accomplices. It was pretty well agreed, and the Whitehead Commission concorded, that the act was the individual work of a sex-crazed, deranged woman who was, however, very possibly a tool of the right-wing underground. Who could risk that sort of implication simply to visit a woman who was doomed anyway? -- even if she was the exFirst Lady.

Dwight offered Carla a cigarette which she refused with a shake of her head. The room was bare except for their two chairs and a small table. Her black hair had lost its lustre. On her small frame hung a seersucker prison dress buttoned to the neck. Her shoes were dull brown and ponderous; they laced up the front -- the final insult to a beautiful and proud woman.

"Dwight?" She played with his cufflink and began to employ the same weapon that had gained her so much in life.

"Yes?" he replied. His voice echoed unpleasantly in the barren room.

"Do you love me?" She drew closer and looked up at him. Her eyes were full and brimming over.

He drew back involuntarily. "Carla, that's an odd question to ask me now. .

"Will you do me a favor?" She took one of his hands in both of hers.

"I'll do what I can..."

"I want my ashes spread on your beach back home. It could have been my home, you know, if you'd..."

"Carla, the trial hasn't even started yet," he countered. "We don't know..."

She gripped his coat savagely, pressed her forehead against his chest and began to cry openly. "They're going to electrocute me, Dwight. Please don't let them, please!"

"I'll do what I can, Carla," he repeated. Dwight felt guilty and deceitful -- he was sworn to do nothing.

She looked up at him, her eyes wide and glazed with panic. "Dwight," she whispered, "help me escape from here. I have a million dollars put away -- think of it -- a million dollars! We could go anywhere, do anything!" She was practically hanging from his coat lapels and her hands were trembling violently. "And Dwight -- the love. You haven't really had love until you've had it with me -- you just wait and see." Breathing hard with her teeth clenched tightly together, she pressed her pelvis tightly against his and tried to kiss him. "You've never had such love..."

Her voice was a barely audible, lilting murmur.

Dwight tore himself away from her, disgusted and repulsed. Many years of growing revulsion had reached its apex. His voice sounded harsh and unreal. "Carla, what do you think I am anyway? You could never buy me with your sex and you know it!" Carla sat down and buried her face in her hands. Dwight rang for the jailer with a savage poke at the button. "And as for your money, I suggest you leave it to the Boy

Scouts!" He immediately regretted that. "I'm sorry, Carla," he said hoarsely. "Do you want me to come back next week?" She nodded assent without looking up.

Dwight drove from the prison unnerved and depressed. He felt partially responsible for the whole terrible mess. Hadn't he introduced Warren to Carla? Shouldn't he have told Warren about her total lack of moral integrity? Couldn't he have done more to influence the President?

* * *

At the trial the prosecution produced photographs showing Carla in various forms of compromise with a dozen different men, including an ex-president. The aging widower had been easy prey. The handsome Polish diplomat, Jaskinski, with whom she was also pictured, Dwight knew to be a Soviet agent. Jasinski testified that Carla had told him she was going to murder the President and then return with him to Poland.

A cyanide gun was produced in evidence and three experts testified that the fingerprints found on it were hers. Material under her fingernails had been "analyzed" and found to be potassium cyanide. This analysis was done over a week after the assassination. Her lawyers did not question the implausibility of this. The case was airtight. The trial lasted ten days. She was sentenced to die by electrocution in sixty days. It wasn't necessary, Dwight thought. Carla died on the day of her conviction. Paralyzed with fear and with her bag of tricks exhausted, Carla offered nothing further in defense of herself.

Finally her mind ceased to register present events. She neither spoke nor ate. She lived in a joyous dream world of the past as the hundreds of lovers trooped before her. She relived in exquisite detail her sexual conquests -- Senators, Ambassadors, gardeners, doctors -- all of them. There were those who wept when she dropped them and those who laughed when she, in turn, wept. She remembered the fat old men who adored her; the sexual marathons with the handsome young bucks, stupid in conversation but deliciously consuming in matters of the flesh; the coxcombs; the effeminate ones; the brutes; the tender ones -- all of them. On and on and over and over it went in a never-ending dream of passion that completely shut out her sickening fear of death.

The press loudly congratulated itself on its coverage of the execution. "The greatest reporting job since the Kennedy assassination," they boasted. Television even brought the shaving of her head and the execution itself into homes all over the world. There was some outcry about bad taste, but the press said that the people had a right to see, read and hear "all the news."

The documentaries were in full swing weeks before the execution. The TV camera focused on the empty chair in the death house. The rich, solemn voice of the narrator gave the history of the modes of execution through the ages -- the camera remained on the chair. "--and, of course, the style of the French Revolution needs no description. The electric chair, which replaced the simple hangman's noose, came into style in 1888. The first criminal executed by this method was William Kemmler at Auburn Prison, on the 6th of August, 1890." The picture changed to an overhead view of the empty electric chair. "It requires about 45 seconds to strap the condemned person into the chair. The initial charge is 2000 volts for from 3 to 4 seconds. About 15 minutes following death, an interesting phenomenon occurs ... the body temperature, instead of dropping from the normal 98.6 degrees Fahrenheit, rises to about 128 degrees..."

The day of the execution arrived and a mesmerized nation watched its television screens as Carla was led in and placed in the chair. The straps and electrodes were applied and the circuit was closed. Her body tensed, then went limp. They convulsed her three more times and then the camera focused on her chest as the prison doctor listened for the heart tones that would indicate life was still present. Then solemnly facing into the camera, the pores of his skin filled with sweat, the doctor announced that his patient was dead.

11. The Underground

Dwight sent his family back to Sarasota soon after Carla was sentenced to die. He stayed on in Washington, until the nightmare was over, to offer Carla what moral support he could. After the execution, he tendered his official resignation and returned to Sarasota.

Dwight had been home a week when Dr. Tom Mahan, his old friend and leader of the Southeastern Underground, came to see him.

He knew what Tom wanted and almost dreaded talking to him.

It was unusually cool for October; a fire burned glowingly in the living room fireplace. The Gulf of Mexico was choppy and gray. Even the sea gulls, squatting on the beach in clusters, seemed despondent. To Dwight and Beth Huckins, life seemed unreal, the past unbelievable and the future nonexistent. The three tenses were jumbled. What could be more important than what had happened? What was happening now that made any difference? Life, during this period of shock, had become an anticlimax.

Dr. Mahan got right to the point. "Huck, the Underground needs you more than ever. No one has the anti-Communist contacts around the country that you have. Are you going to join us?"

Dwight, his hands in his pockets, stared at the fire. "Tom, I've been through a lot. I've witnessed the assassination of the President of the United States. I have seen them execute a woman, whom I'd known since I was sixteen, for a crime she didn't commit. We were lucky to get out of Washington alive -- just how much can one family take?" Mahan, balding in front, sipped his Bourbon and soda and said nothing. The firelight reflected brightly on his rimless glasses. Thomas Mahan, M.D., an ear, nose and throat specialist, looked like anything but a guerrilla fighter. But this tall, frail, scholarly-looking man had engineered the complete collapse of the UN occupation of Atlanta, only a year before. Although he had commanded 500 men in that operation, only Dwight and a few others knew it.

The UN troops in Atlanta, under command of Russian General Dimitri Lebedev, had been unstable and undisciplined. The Army was mostly black African and half-breed South American. They were woefully inept marksmen; no match for the squirrel-shooting Southerners. The Underground, under the command of Tom Mahan, played on the superstitions of the Africans, and using a liberal dose of Southern humor, made a shambles of the entire UN operation.

General Lebedev had, for weeks, been receiving tips from informers (who were actually underground operatives), that the Underground had large caches of arms on Kennesaw Mountain. The first UN sortie sent to investigate the rumors was a truckload of dark-skinned troops. Just before a sharp bend at the foot of the mountain, the truck came upon a woman lying by the side of the road. She yelled for help. It was a Negress, dressed in tattered UN blue. The truck stopped and the driver and all 20 of the giggling, helmeted Negro soldiers, disobeying orders, tumbled out. Suddenly the girl rolled over, pulled a machine gun from the ditch beside her and at point blank range, neatly dispatched them all. The next morning a light plane flew over the UN headquarters in downtown Atlanta and, with a resounding clatter, showered the building and surrounding area with the battered helmets of the dead UN soldiers.

Three days later, two truckloads of troops went out to find the cache of arms on Kennesaw Mountain. Again there was a body just before the sharp bend in the mountain road. A UN soldier, sitting on a front fender, pumped 20 rounds into the still form. The troops gleefully disembarked. The form was a dummy. But the Americans hiding in wait among the rocks on both sides of the road, were not dummies. All but one of the UN soldiers was killed in the devastating crossfire. The survivor was sent back, naked except for his blue and white UN helmet, to tell his story.

General Lebedev, enraged, decided to clean out Kennesaw Mountain once and for all. Taking personal command, Lebedev led his two thousand troops in an attack from four sides of the mountain with heavy artillery and tanks. Not a guerrilla, a pistol, or rifle was found. The Underground group was by then in Decatur, 20 miles on the other side of Atlanta, raiding General Lebedev's country mansion and kidnapping his fat daughter.

General Lebedev announced that Atlanta, unlike New York, did not appear to be ready for UN protection. Even the Southern Negroes whom they had been sent to protect, he said despairingly, didn't appreciate them and had joined the Underground.

General Lebedev announced the departure of his "peace-keeping" forces from Atlanta, hoping that the announcement would quiet things down. But, much to his dismay, he and his UN troops had to fight their way back north through Mahan's guerrilla army. At the South Carolina line another guerrilla band picked them up and harassed them all the way to Richmond. The General arrived in New York with a motley crew of six hundred. The welcome there was less than enthusiastic. The Underground had sent his daughter back ahead of him, shaken but unharmed. Her only memento of the experience was the tattoo they had put across her massive chest: GOD BLESS AMERICA, in red and blue letters. General Lebedev was sent back to Russia for "reassignment." He was never heard of again.

Dwight Huckins, recalling Tom Mahan's fantastic accomplishments, felt a sense of guilt for refusing Tom's request. But Mahan had caught him at a bad moment. Only that morning Dwight had received the first threatening phone call since returning home. Tom Mahan may have done courageous things, but unlike Dwight, he was completely unknown to the enemy. "Tom, I just want to practice medicine and lead a reasonably normal life again. Remember, I know too much -- I am exposed; you are not." Tom Mahan set his drink down. "Huck, I never thought I would see the day when you would worry about your neck instead of..."

"Damn it, Tom," Dwight jumped to his feet, "I just can't seem to make you understand." He began to shout. "My children were spat upon at school. In Georgetown, Beth had her tires slashed; she has received threatening phone calls, usually in filthy language, and every day now she wonders if I'll come home alive. Tom, we've *had* it." Dwight poked at the fire viciously. "It's hopeless. Americans don't deserve freedom. They've seen the Communists kill two of our presidents and they're letting the UN take over the country. Look at Hawaii. The Chinese have just taken it over at a cost to us of 10,000 men, women and children. Wade Hampton Trotter, the best general since MacArthur, is in disgrace because they've blamed the whole mess on him -

- and the American people are falling for it! Downtown today I saw six drunken UN soldiers. They were black and had rings in their noses. They were shoving people off the streets and the police pretended not to see. So what the hell can we do?"

Dr. Mahan stood up and tossed his cigar into the fire. "I guess I'd better go, Huck."

"Good night, Tom -- I'm sorry."

After Dr. Mahan left, Dwight Huckins paced the floor. He knew that he couldn't stop fighting, not for long. What sense was there in going on if you didn't at least try? He wanted a little time to clear his head and heart, but they needed him *now*. Mahan had said that something big was brewing. A lot of flying activity had been reported below the 26th parallel and the Underground feared some sort of air strike. Where they would strike was anybody's guess. The Underground would need communications to keep the country together if something really big happened. But how? The mails were too slow and heavily censored by UNIFLIB (UN Free Flow of Information Bureau). The UN's jamming operation made radio difficult and unreliable.

Dwight waited long enough for Tom to reach home and then called him. "Tom, I've got an idea."

"Huck, my boy, you've always got an idea --shoot!" Tom Mahan was immediately rejuvenated.

Dwight outlined a plan for a telephone network across the country. With his contacts from coast to coast, he could, in an emergency, telephone vital information to key cities in a prearranged code. These key people would in turn fan the messages out by telephone through their appointed areas. This would, in effect, greatly expand and strengthen the skeleton system now operating and would enable them to reach every town and hamlet in the United States more quickly. The enemy often moved with the speed of light and every second saved was important. If they had had this improved set-up when Silverbright was assassinated, perhaps they could have avoided most of the hysteria and tragedies that followed.

The United Nations had developed the science of propaganda to the point where its cybernetic warfare arm, UNIFLIB, could strike like lightning across the land inducing paralysis through fear, narcosis through carefully spun fairy tales about peace, or deadly rage and a lynching psychosis against a selected enemy of the United Nations. Eventually the people would realize that they had been led down a blind alley or induced to commit an outrage against one of their own. But the truth always lagged far enough behind the deed to be valueless. Their mistake would be quickly forgotten as the giant UNIFLIB propaganda octopus seized the people's minds and led them toward another chimera of lies, false hopes, terror or simply into a fog of utter helplessness.

"Tom, I might be optimistic, but I think I could cover the entire United States in two hours. What do you think?"

"Dwight, I think it's great. Why don't you get on with it? We may need it sooner than you think!" Dwight agreed that he would. "Incidentally, Huck," said Tom, "our next meeting is Saturday. Will you come?"

"O.K., Tom -- you win."

12. Checkmate

Tom Mahan's appearance belied his military experience. This tall, rather frail man, with his rimless glasses, looked more like an English teacher than a guerrilla fighter. But Mahan was a graduate of The Citadel, one of the nation's finest military colleges. After The Citadel he went to medical school and a year later was called into the Korean War.

Serving as battalion surgeon under General Wade Hampton Trotter, he and the general became warm friends. Trotter recognized in Mahan an enviable quality; the ability to be proficient in two entirely distinct fields of endeavor. In this case it was medicine and military tactics. He saw in Mahan the making of a truly great military surgeon. General Trotter was a widower; his only son was killed in the last days of World War II. Major Tom Mahan quickly became the surrogate for that son and, as they faced the enemy through the dark Korean nights, the father-son relationship deepened.

After their frequent chess games, Trotter and Mahan would discuss world affairs and especially the Communist conspiracy. Under Trotter's tutelage, Mahan became well-versed and, consequently, very alarmed about the degree of Communist infiltration and control of the United States Government.

Mahan's awakening had started early in their relationship -- one wet night in a soggy, lamp-lit medical aid tent just behind the front lines. There was an occasional "ba-ruum" in the distance as the Chinese Reds kept the pressure on. The gas lamp overhead swung slightly as a stray shell landed nearby. The men, concentrating on their game, hardly noticed. The general studied his protege, who was bleakly surveying an unpromising array of knights, bishops and pawns. Trotter had been waiting for an opportunity to probe Mahan's knowledge on the origins of and forces behind this undeclared war. Mahan adjusted his glasses and cautiously moved a bishop.

"Checkmate," the general declared.

Tom leaned back in his chair. Their matches brought an expert against the master and the results were almost always the same. "Well, General, I knew I was done in six moves ago but I wasn't quite sure why --what did I do wrong this time ?"

General Hampton chuckled, causing his pointed waxed mustache to twitch mischievously. "Everything, Tom," he teased, "but your mistakes are becoming more sophisticated every day."

"Well, thank *you*, Sir. That's very comforting indeed!" Tom grinned, took off his glasses and rubbed his eyes.

General Trotter picked up the chessmen and carefully placed them in their felt-lined box. "Tom, did you know that our government has absolutely no control over the conduct of this war -- that the Communists, through the UN, are running both sides ?"

Mahan, obviously startled, could think of no intelligent reply.

"You've never heard of a little Chinese rat named Sam Yen, have you ?" Trotter asked.

"No, I don't think so -- why?"

"Well, Sammy Yen, we've found out through G-2 informants in Hong Kong, is a Soviet agent. He runs a fur store there as a cover. This little baldheaded worm has been scurrying back and forth between Hong Kong and here carrying *our war plans*, which he obtains from a UN courier, to General Vasiliev, the Russian cut-throat who's directing those guns you hear out there."

Stunned, Tom thought for a moment. "And how does he get away with *that?*"

"He comes with UN credentials and so goes anywhere he damn pleases. We can't stop him -- treaty law and all that." Trotter put the chess box on a shelf above the coffee urn. "How about a cup of coffee, Tom?"

"Yes, please." Tom pushed on, his temper mounting. "Well why don't we stop him anyway, and who's responsible in the UN? This is treason!"

"Now Tom, settle down. I've only half finished my story." He looked at his reflection in Tom's stainless steel sterilizer and patted the thick panniculus of fat under his belt. "You'd think a guy would lose weight on our diet -- can't seem to lose a pound."

Handing Mahan his cup of coffee, he peered out through the tent flap at the glow of war in the distance. "Do you know where Vasiliev was before he started matching wits with us out here ?" the general queried.

"No sir."

"Well, I'll tell you. He was at the UN as Soviet representative of the UN Military Staff Committee -- *that's* where he was."

Mahan, obviously shaken, then asked the logical question: "And who in the UN is making our war plans now?"

"The man who is now UN Undersecretary for Security Council Affairs -- that's the guy who runs this war -- is none other than Constantin E. Zinchenko, another Russian Communist."

"My God, this is fantastic," Tom exclaimed. "'What..."

"Wait!" Placing his hand on Tom's shoulder, the general cut him short. He thought he had heard the faint sound of a bugle in the distance. His sloping shoulders tensed. Listening for the bugle, the tips of his waxed mustache seemed to probe for sound. The bugle call came again more clearly through the night and the general's ears went back like an agitated stallion as he turned to steel and exploded into action. "It's a surprise attack -- another human wave -- let's move!" The general was out of the tent, into his jeep and heading for the front lines almost before Tom could put down his cup.

The UN forgotten, Tom grabbed the phone and ordered all corpsmen to report to the aid tent on the double. He would be busy tonight with the torn limbs and shattered lives of young American citizens fighting in a war that was rigged against them.

* * *

Tom's friendship with General Wade Hampton Trotter changed the course of his life. By the end of the Korean War, Tom had definitely decided to make a career of the Army. What better way could a man serve his country than by ministering to the medical and psychological needs of America's fighting men? Trotter had convinced him of the need to educate the soldier about Communism and what America stood for. The general had given him a thorough grounding in the sinister forces that threatened the United States both from within its borders and from without. By the time Trotter and Mahan parted for different posts, Mahan had a thorough knowledge of the tyranny in the labor movement, the perfidy of the U.S. Supreme Court, and the subversive forces at work in the mental health movement, education and the nation's churches. He determined, with the general's enthusiastic blessing, to transmit this knowledge to the men under his command. The shocking revelation, after the Korean War, that many captured Americans went over to the Communist side made him all the more determined to do his share in reviving the failing American spirit of patriotism.

But Mahan, as would General Trotter later, ran head-on into forces within the U.S. Government that wanted "world citizenship" and not love of country taught to the American soldier. Lt. Colonel Mahan was aghast and incredulous when, after a number of years of educating those under his command about Communism, with the approval of his commanding officers, he received an adverse fitness report.

"Lt. Colonel Mahan is alert and his professional judgment is outstanding," the report said. "However, since being at this command, he has had progressive interest and activity in his own pilgrimage of fighting Communism to the point that he is an extremist in his rightist beliefs. This officer seems to have difficulty keeping his identity as an Army Officer divorced from his personal anti-Communist crusade. Because of his anti-Communist zeal, and his obvious antagonism toward the United Nations, he has been the subject of additional security investigations,,,"

Thoroughly confounded by this reversal in policy, Tom wrote his reply:

"It was with a sense of shock that I read my fitness report of 15 January, 1960. Upon accepting my commission as an Army Officer, I took an oath to support the Constitution of the United States -- not the United Nations Charter. The anti-Communist activities mentioned in my fitness report were merely a continuation of similar activities that had been encouraged at previous duty stations. Since it is the sworn duty of every officer to defend his country against all enemies, and since the Communists are acknowledged enemies of the United States, it follows that every officer should exert every effort to inform those under his command of the dangers of Communism, both foreign and domestic.

"Believing that I can work for my country more effectively as a private citizen, without the restraints now being imposed upon those in the military service, it is with sadness and a deep feeling of responsibility to my country that I submit my request for release from the United States Army.~,

Mahan was released forthwith. After surgical specialty training, he returned to Sarasota, opened his medical office and immediately began organizing the Southeastern section of the MacArthur Legion.

13. The Men From UNIT

General Wade Hampton Trotter, both the hero and the villain of the Hawaiian Invasion, was in Washington to clear his name of charges of incompetence. The General awoke at 7 AM, as was his custom. He shuffled, barefoot and in his underwear, to his hotel bathroom. Always acutely aware of the weather (it had played a great part in his military life) he noted at his window that the day promised to be clear and crisp.

General Trotter peered into the bathroom mirror, gingerly poking at the bags and dark circles under his eyes. "A little sun would help that," he mused. He touched up the points of his waxed mustache by rolling them between thumb and finger. Most military commanders have some distinguishing characteristic. MacArthur had his pipe and gold braid hat; Patton his pearl-handled pistols. Trotter was not especially fond of the mustache but he considered it to be an important identifying characteristic and a necessary symbol. He had an endomorphic body type and a balding head. Thus, he did not cut the military figure commensurate with his brilliant accomplishments: he never had. His was a brilliant mind trapped in an unprepossessing body. All of his life he had fought the nickname "Pudgy" and the Prussian mustache was one of his defenses.

Although a vain man, Trotter was a masterful tactician and a dedicated patriot. His penetrating blue eyes, peering through his puffy eyelids, missed very little. He was an expert on guerrilla warfare and, contrary to his general physical appearance, he had the cunning and agility of a mountain lion.

Being deeply concerned about the grip the United Nations had on the country, Trotter saw his duty clearly: After the hearing he would join the anti-Communist underground whether he was successful in clearing his name or not. His effectiveness as a military commander in the American Army was obviously at an end but he wanted to clear his name, if possible, before resigning. After resigning he would take the only course left to him. He would accept the offer of his old friend, Tom Mahan, and the other leaders of the MacArthur Legion to take command of the underground army.

General Trotter knew what he would be up against if he took command of the revolutionary forces: the leading of patriotic, willing but undisciplined men who were poorly fed, unpaid, and underarmed. He would be up against not only the military might of the United Nations, but its propaganda machine, UNIFLIB, which would attempt to turn the people against the underground army. And, of course, there would be a heavy price on his head as a "peace criminal." But Wade Hampton Trotter had a sense of history; he saw clearly the parallels between George Washington's beleaguered army and the one he intended to command. If General Washington could win with a group of untrained American patriots then so could he.

Trotter had provoked the wrath of the Peace Department brass at the time of the UN takeover of Brownsville in May of 1978. At that time he had remarked at a cocktail party in West Germany that "Seneca acts more like the President than Silverbright does." Being also an outspoken foe of the United Nations, he taught the troops under his command that their allegiance was to the United States Constitution and not to the United Nations Charter which, he said, "was designed by the Communists as an instrument of global conquest."

His remark about Seneca evoked a loud and unremitting campaign in the press for his removal as Commander of UNEPO (United Nations European Peace Organization). His anti-U.N. remarks added fuel to the fire and resulted in an official reprimand for "conduct unbecoming a United Nations Peace Commander." He was removed from his post and transferred to Hawaii soon thereafter. The Hawaiian invasion began four months after he had assumed the command there.

Fighting the waves of Red Chinese infantry under impossible odds, the General had saved as many Americans as he could. Because he knew that torture and death would be the fate of any white woman or child left on the Islands, he commandeered every boat of any size, loaded the refugees aboard, and sent them toward the mainland awaiting air rescue. The next day a storm struck. Only five per cent of the castaways were saved in operations directed from California. A week later General Trotter and his decimated garrison were airlifted to the U.S. under a UN-directed truce.

The blame for the entire Hawaiian disaster was laid at the feet of General Wade Hampton Trotter and he was editorially crucified for "sending thousands of women and children to a watery grave."

Trotter averred that the invasion of Hawaii was planned from United Nations headquarters in New York "in collusion with the captive U.S. Government," and that it was a plot designed to turn Hawaii over to the Chinese Communists and concurrently to destroy him.

A young cryptographer in the White House confirmed this in a report to a newsman whom he trusted, but who was, in actuality, an agent for UNIT (United Nations Intelligence Team). He revealed to the reporter that Washington officials had broken the Chinese code and had known of the Hawaiian invasion plans by the Chinese a week in advance. Seneca, UNAssistant to the President, had ordered the intelligence suppressed. He claimed that it was only "a military probing action" and that if General Trotter were apprised of it he would "only aggravate the situation with his awful temper."

All UN departments were infiltrated with anti-Communist intelligence operatives; UNIT was no exception. UNIT double agents immediately transmitted the cryptographer's confession to friends of General Trotter.

The General, encouraged by this intelligence, had issued an immediate press release demanding a hearing to clear his name. But he made the error of also demanding that all personnel in White House Communications be subpoenaed for questioning concerning the Hawaiian disaster of November 11th, 1978. This latter demand tipped his hand and thus destroyed any chance he may have had of a fair hearing. It also sealed the fate of his star witness..."

* * *

The little newspaper vender who held forth at one of New York's busiest intersections was part of the human flotsam that one sees peddling newspapers the world over. He had never heard of General Wade Hampton Trotter and probably never would. But their lives were about to have a dramatic, though fleeting, common interest. Eddie McCabe's legs were ludicrously short; his arms almost touched the ground. His head was huge and his hair laid over the back of his filthy collar. He wore his cap off to one side. As he hawked his papers, his mouth would become grotesque and mobile. He prided himself on having the loudest voice in New York City. He carried a huge bundle of papers under his left arm and one paper in his right hand which he flailed and twisted in every conceivable direction to attract the attention of the elegant passersby. As he peeled off the headlines, he would add little touches of his own to pique the interest of his potential customers.

Although Eddie had little power of intellection, he had a keen sort of animal intelligence characteristic of his breed. He missed very little that passed his busy corner of the world and he was fond of making what he considered sage comments about the behavior of his fellow human beings as he saw them from his vantage point. His was an intelligence of the moment. The next day he couldn't recall whom he had seen or what he had seen of life's panorama. Life was one day long and it never occured to him to think of yesterday or tomorrow.

Today was the kind of day he liked best. It was very cold but the sky was crystal clear. He loved the magnificent spikes of concrete, stone, steel and glass known as Manhattan. It saddened him when he could not see the tips of these man-made obelisks. When the smog or clouds cut off the tops of the skyscrapers, his world was compressed and it subconsciously reminded him that his little body was compressed and ugly.

As he bawled out the day's headlines, he automatically classified the two well—dressed young men across the street. His bird-like little eyes scanned them and quickly catalogued their salient features; felt hats, well fitting pin-striped suits, watch with metal band on the left wrists and identification bracelets on the right wrists. "Government men," he summarized. "I wonder what they're doing here?" He forgot them as he sold a paper to a well-furred dowager with artificial blonde hair. His monstrous hand, furfuraceous and fiery red from the cold, quickly deposited her 50 cents in his change apron and then dropped her change back into her gloved hand.

"Hi ya, Stumpy." An acquaintance greeted him and hurried by pushing a large garment carrier before him. Eddie mumbled a greeting as he turned to sell another paper to a young student who struggled with an armload of books as he fumbled for his change. He looked up from his change apron and again noticed the young "government men~~ across the street. They appeared tense and were looking up at the tall building adjoining the one in front of which they were standing. Eddie's gaze immediately shot upward and he was frozen with surprise as he witnessed a man struggling with two other men on a ledge of about the 20th floor. The figure seemed to clutch desperately for the wall of the building as his feet slid off the ledge and he plummeted downward. Dropping his papers, Eddie was halfway across the street when the body struck the pavement with a shattering sound like the crushing of a grapefruit hurled against a wall. The young man's head had been smashed into a hemisphere. It looked like a gargoyle with the tongue protruding and the one eye that remained looking up blankly at the sky.

A crowd quickly gathered around the gruesome remains. Eddie, lost in the big crowd, listened to the comments. "A suicide --he could've hit someone." Smug and indifferent, the man shoved his hands into his coat pockets and elbowed his way back through the crowd. A young woman, her hand over her mouth, exclaimed, "He's so young --isn't it horrible ?" Two elderly ladies exchanged their views: "The poor boy must have been in terrible trouble to do such a thing--' what a tragedy for one so young."

Eddie, taking in these remarks, could stand it no longer. "It ain't suicide!" he exclaimed. "I seen it myself. By Jesus, he was pushed!" No one paid any attention to him and he started jumping up and down, angered because of the lack of attention. "By Jesus, I seen it. It ain't a suicide --I seen him pushed -- two men pushed him out. I seen it, I seen it!"

The two young men were suddenly at Eddie's side. They appeared undisturbed and friendly. The taller of the two put his hand on Eddie's shoulder and smiled. "Better take it easy, Eddie. Do you realize your papers are blowing all over the street ?"

Eddie looked up and his face became pale. "How did ya know my name? -- I don't want no trouble."

"We're not going to cause you any trouble, Eddie. Come on, let's get those newspapers." The two men escorted Eddie back across the street, one on each side. An ambulance siren whined in the distance and the police began breaking up the crowd. Eddie's papers had blown in every direction and were quite beyond salvaging. "It looks like your papers are a lost cause, Eddie."

Eddie's animal cunning signaled that he was in trouble. "Ain't nothin' -- the next edition'll be out in half an hour and I'll make it up." He looked uneasily from one man to the other. The shorter of the two men smiled benignly at Eddie but he never spoke and never took his hands out of his overcoat. The tall one who did the talking was the boss, Eddie reasoned, as he tried desperately to think of some excuse to get away. "I made $40 yesterday so it don't mean nothin' -- I gotta get my tail over to the office or they'll can me sure 'n hell."

The tall one, still smiling, casually took a leather bound card case out of his coat pocket and briefly flashed it at Eddie. Eddie paled and began to tremble as he noted the bright purple letters on the card: "UNIT."

"I didn't do nuthin' -- I gotta go -- I don't want no trouble!" He started backing away and the shorter man took him by the arm.

The tall one took out his wallet, picked out a crisp $100 bill and handed it to Eddie. "This ought to cover your losses, Eddie. Why don't you just forget about what you saw awhile ago?"

Eddie's face flushed and he broke into a grin revealing a line of nicotine-stained pegs. "I didn't see nuthin'," he said as he quickly pocketed the hundred dollar bill. "I don't want no trouble and I didn't see nuthin' -- you guys comin' back?"

"No, Eddie," said the tall one, looking intently at him. "We're not coming back --unless we have to." The smile had left his face as he peered down at the dirty little man.

Eddie instinctively grasped the significance of the remark. "I ain't gonna talk. I ain't gonna say nuthin'. Don't you worry about old Eddie, the Stump. He can keep a secret and he don't want to get in trouble with *you* guys."

The two men, now unsmiling, surveyed their quarry. "Always remember that, Eddie." Without waiting for him to remark, they walked briskly down the street and got into a black car in the next block. They made a U-turn and were soon out of sight.

Eddie rubbed his hands in glee and walked down the street as fast as his little legs would carry him toward his favorite bar. The crushed body on the sidewalk behind was already forgotten. That evening he would be peddling the news which in glaring banner would tell of the "suicide" of an obscure cryptographer who worked somewhere in Washington. Eddie's lips would be sealed, partly from fear of the "government men" and partly because his brain simply did not store anything beyond the latest headline. A few days later the news would break as to who the cryptographer really was but the fact that he was a White House employee would mean little or nothing to Eddie as the original event would be too far beyond his memory span.

With the elimination of this witness, General Trotter clearly recognized the hopelessness of trying to clear his name. He attacked the administration in a press conference in which he stated that, in his opinion, the cryptographer was murdered to cover up the greatest scandal in history. His statement was buried in the back pages of some newspapers; it was not carried at all by most of them. General Trotter resigned his commission and wasted no time in contacting Underground leaders. He was soon in command of all underground operations.

14. Bombing of Boston

(DECEMBER 7, 1979)

Dwight's renewed association with Tom Mahan gave him fresh strength, new courage. When the Huckinses first returned to Sarasota, they had been appalled by the ignorance and apathy of their friends. Dwight and Beth were considered "a little peculiar" on the subject of Communism, and this set them apart. Dwight tried to convince anyone who would listen to him that the United States was becoming, a piece at a time, an occupied country. Something had to be done about South Florida *fast* or they would all finish out their lives as Communist slaves. However, there had not been an incident at the 26th parallel, in Florida or Texas, for over a year and business was good all over the country. Dwight soon realized that he was considered a bore on the subject of Communism and so he usually avoided discussing it.

But occasionally he would become enraged and create a scene: "Say, Dwight, was Carla really going to fly the coop with that handsome Polack?" Before he realized what he was doing, Dwight had the man across the bar and almost broke his neck. Invitations to parties became infrequent, but it didn't matter for he and Beth had long since ceased to enjoy them.

Time passed quickly. Dwight was constantly at meetings, some medical, some clandestine. Beth never asked about the latter for she knew that Dwight had become an active part of Tom Mahan's section of General Trotter's underground.

Their friends had changed, but their favorite spot in the world, their Crescent Beach home on the Gulf of Mexico, had not. They really needed little else. The Huckins family was close-knit. Martha was now 15, blonde and beautiful. In spite of her parents' reputation as "alarmists," she had many young admirers. David, 13, was mature for his age. He had inherited the integrity and courage of his father.

Fall passed, then winter quickly gave way to spring and suddenly it was sailboat time again. Each afternoon about four o'clock, Beth and the children would ready their 15-foot Flying Fin racing boat. At five, barring emergencies, Dwight would arrive home and they would push the little sailboat into the Gulf. When they returned, the sun would be dipping deep into the sea. They would eat supper in their bathing suits on the screened porch, with the rhythmic rush of the Gulf for music. It was traditional for Marty and Dave to alternate the saying of grace for the evening meal. Marty folded her hands in her lap and bowed her blonde head: "Bless us, Oh Lord, for these our gifts which we are about to receive, from Thy bounty, in Christ's name -- Amen." The Huokins family had found happiness far greater than that found in the average home. Knowing that the future held grave challenges, they were able to enjoy more intensely what they had.

Midway through dinner the telephone rang. Beth answered it and returned to the table. "It was Roberta Larkin. She's invited us to a party next Saturday night."

"Well, will wonders never cease!" Dwight said. "You mean we are no longer social outcasts or is she just looking for some comedy relief? -- you know, doomsday sandwich boards and all that."

"Now Dwight, Roberta has been very nice."

"Why don't you go, Dad?" Martha asked. "You and Mother haven't been out in ages."

"I'll babysit," David added with a grin.

Beth looked at her husband. "Why don't we go, Dwight?" she urged. "It just might be fun."

Dwight looked seriously at the intent faces around the table. "All those in favor of Doctor and Mrs. Huckins going to this drunken brawl, raise their right hands." Three hands went up. "It looks as though I'm outvoted."

* * *

Because the town was quite an art center, Sarasota's parties always produced a conglomerate and colorful group. Roberta Larkin's was no exception. Dwight listened with disgust but pretended not to hear as the one-legged sculptor with the bushy beard expostulated on world government. "In the march of history, man is constantly groping for a better world. The inevitable historical process is leading us to the age of peace under world law." He gesticulated grandiosly as he talked. His thin, languid blonde companion looked bored. She leaned against the wall and surveyed the party for someone to flirt with. Dwight sat at the bar and slowly turned his glass between his palms. The bearded one, leaning an elbow against the wall continued, "The UN peace force will soon wipe out the remaining jingoistic fanatics in this country and relegate the U.S. Constitution to where it belongs -- the outhouse of history."

Beth put her hand on Dwight's arm. His tensing jaw muscles indicated the fuse was burning short. The bearded slob was warming to his subject. "The Christians have to suffer, you know. The masochist bastards want to keep the world a Goddamn hell-hole so they can suffer their way into a higher seat in heaven." His face became red. He began to shout.

His sallow companion, now alarmed, took his glass. He had slopped half its contents onto his greasy sweat shirt. "For Christ's sake shut up, Steiner," she said, "everybody's watching you." He tried to light a cigarette, couldn't find the end, and threw it on the floor.

He reeled toward the bathroom, leaning on his frail companion. "We're going to let all the God-lovers suffer together," he shouted. "We're gonna stuff the Christians, the Jews and the Buddhists into the same outhouse and pour kerosene over it." His speech was slurred and barely intelligible. "They can stink and suffer all they want. The bastards..." Julius Steiner, sculptor, stumbled toward the bathroom, fell and lost consciousness.

"Come on, Dwight. Let's get something to eat." Beth urged. They crossed to the dining room, stepping around the outstretched hulk on the floor.

Dwight picked some boiled shrimp from the bowl on the buffet table. Tokay Wren, five feet eleven inches tall, copper-colored and big boned, was in line in front of him. Tokay had prominent clavicles and very high prominent cheekbones. In fact, all of Tokay Wren's attributes were prominent. She was a full-blooded Cherokee Indian whose daddy had found oil in Oklahoma. Tokay at parties presented an impression of giddy abandon. But she had an intellectual depth and patriotic fervor that would have surprised most people. Having had Tokay as a patient, Dwight had an opportunity to sound out her political attitudes. He knew what most Sarasotans did not: Tokay Wren was a beautifully packaged piece of dynamite just waiting to be detonated for her country when and if called upon.

After a number of visits to his office and a cementing of their friendship, Dwight could no longer resist asking her about the large, gray, black and white feather that she always wore somewhere in her hair. Only a flamboyant personality with figure and name to match could get away with it. On Tokay Wren it looked perfectly natural. Dwight had quickly detected that she wore the feather to fit her mood. During that certain phase of the ovarian cycle, the feather would be pointed downward, backward and would be hardly noticeable. When she felt gay and giddy, the plume would be placed straight up at the crown of her satin-black hair and she would become the epitome of the beautiful Indian princess.

"Tokay," Dwight had asked during an office visit as he took the blood pressure cuff from around her arm, "why do you always wear that feather in your hair? I'm not being inquisitive, you understand," he added with a grin, "just nosey."

"My dear doctor, haven't you figured *that* out yet?" Her copper-colored hands gripped the examining table as she tilted her head to one side and looked at him with a feigned perplexity and a mischievous grin. (It was one of her straight-up feather days).

"Well," he studied her with an elbow in hand and finger to his lips, "you *could* be a

Cherokee spy but on the other hand... I've got it. Your father's name was Eagle's Feather!"

Tokay's flame-red lips parted in a wide grin, revealing perfect teeth that appeared startlingly white in contrast to her bronze complexion. "Right! My father was a patriot and a capitalist long before he noticed the oily taste to his well water and he told me all about Aesop when I was only eight --he was proud of his name. He would say that he was hatched from an American Eagle's egg and..."

"Wait a minute; wait a minute," Dwight pleaded, "let's go back a little -- what's this Aesop business?"

"Aesop's Fables -- silly," she chided him, "don't you know the story of the eagle's feather?"

"No, but I have a feeling I'm about to."

"It goes like this." She was suddenly serious of countenance and Dwight knew that Tokay Wren was speaking from the heart. "A hunter shot an eagle with an arrow. As the noble bird fell, he saw that the shaft of the arrow had been winged with one of his own feathers. 'Oh,' said the dying eagle, 'why is it that we so often give our enemies the means of our own destruction?' That's from Aesop's Fable called 'The Eagle and the Arrow,' written around 550 B.C. My father was betrayed by a member of his own family when he was a young man -- just as our country is being betrayed from within today. So *now* do you see?" She tilted her head the other way and, with a quizzical expression, looked at him as though she were trying to impart knowledge to an unintelligent child.

"Yes, Tokay," he replied, obviously struck by the intensity of her emotion, "I understand perfectly -- and I'm glad I asked."

"I like everyone to know where I stand," she said, "especially great patriots like you." Dwight, embarrassed, had quickly changed the subject back to medicine.

* * *

"Oh, Doctor Huckins," Tokay exclaimed as she dipped into the potato salad, "isn't this a perfectly swinging party?" Without waiting for an answer she plunged on. "Say, do you do plastic surgery? I have this friend who is divorced and she has an absolutely dreamy figure except for her breasts -- gourds -- just gourds. Can't something be done about that?" She put some potato salad on his plate without asking if he wanted it. "Having babies did it to her. Mine are still all right because I haven't had babies."

Tokay had learned to take no more than one drink at parties. If she did, her royal Indian blood would flow too freely and her yard long black braid of hair would come alive. As she tossed her head in animated speech, it would as likely as not slap a guest in the face or drag through the punch bowl. Staying with her usual one cocktail, the glistening braid would hang sedately in the middle of her smooth, golden brown back.

Dr. Huckins munched his shrimp, contem' plating the big bronze frame with a mixture of amusement and male appreciation. Her off-the-shoulder dress covered her big sexy body like an onion skin. "Well, Tokay," he said, "the answer to your first question is yes. The answer to your second question is no and the answer to your third question is yes."

Tokay giggled, "Oh, Dr. Huckins, you're a riot. Now, I've forgotten what I asked you!"

"I'll tell you what you do, Tokay." He placed his empty plate on a side table. "Why don't you make up some questions to fit my answers? Beth and I will dance and when we come back, you can tell us what we talked about."

Tokay hooted with amusement, "Oh, Doctor, you *are* a riot!"

The dance floor was crowded. Dwight held Beth close. The amusing interchange with Tokay filled Beth with warmth and wiped away the unpleasant Steiner episode. It was good to see Dwight's sense of humor survive all onslaughts. The crowd had become subdued. The music was soft and sweet. She drew closer and whispered in his ear. "Darling, let's not stay too late. Tokay may look better, but I'll bet she isn't."

Dwight chuckled, "You know, I'll bet you're right!"

Beth drew her head away, "now what do you mean by *that?*" They looked at each other and laughed. There were having a wonderful time.

"Oh, Lawd, Lawd, have mercy!" The Negro maid, temporarily white, came running in from the kitchen. The music stopped and they tried to calm her, but to no avail. The radio in the kitchen was now blaring loudly and everyone could hear:

> "It has been confirmed that Boston has been struck by an atomic weapon. The source of the explosion and the extent of the damage is not yet known."

The radio was silent for a moment. Only the sobbing of the maid and a murmured "God help us" broke the pall of gloom.

> "Here is another bulletin. Earlier reports of the complete eradication by atomic explosion of the greater Boston area are confirmed. A radio station in Springfield, Massachusetts, reports that nothing remains standing in the 50-square-mile area that a moment ago was Boston.
>
> "Here is a direct report by Willard Watkins in Lawrence, Massachusetts: Boston, Massachusetts, proud and traditional, is now radio-active dust. Witnesses from as far as 100 miles away are practically unanimous in their description of that incredible moment: white light, followed by a tremble and a sound as if the earth had split in two. And then a tremendous wind rushing from all points of the compass *toward* Boston -- as if the Almighty were trying to breathe

the breath of life into the striken city. This is Willard Watkins, Lawrence, Massachusetts.

"And now a bulletin from Washington. Central Intelligence Agency officials report that rumors of a plot by rightist groups to provoke war with Russia and China by the atomic destruction of an American city have been commonplace in recent months Several suspects in the New England area have already been picked up."

A number of the guests looked uneasily at Dr. and Mrs. Huckins. Stunned and sobered couples began to leave quietly. As with the murder of President Kennedy sixteen years before, this was a Communist assassination. But this time it was the assassination of an entire city. Dwight doubted that the Kremlin had given the order for the bombing. Rather, he suspected that the pilot of the plane dropping its cargo of mass death was a Red Chinese and that this act was the climax of the struggle that had been going on for years between the Soviet Union and Red China as to the best means of conquering the Free World. The Red Chinese had been maintaining for the past five years that because America had adopted a program of unilateral disarmament and because of the success of Communist infiltration in high places in the U.S. government, *the United States would be helpless in the face of direct physical attack.* If the Red Chinese could get away with such an outrage as the bombing of Boston it could well tip the scales in their favor: the Red Chinese strategy of *direct attack* would then become the modus operandi of Sino-Soviet aggression and world conquest.

> "And here is another bulletin. The White House, Washington. President Gunther has announced that there is absolutely no evidence, we repeat, *no evidence* of any outside power being involved in the Boston atrocity. He said that the atmosphere of hate generated by extremists had now shown itself in full flower with this tragedy. He urged all Americans to practice moderation in this moment of crisis and to have faith in the United Nations. The President was in immediate contact with Chairman Prusakova of Russia and the UN Secretary General Tai Lo. They have offered every assistance, and UN disaster teams are already on the scene at the disaster area."

In spite of the propaganda barrage against the anti-Communists, some incontrovertible facts became known almost immediately. These facts reached Dr. Huckins within hours and his "telephone grapevine," the only reliable source of news left to the American people, went into operation across the country.

An ancient World War II bomber aircraft, a converted B-24 with Cuban markings, had crash-landed in the Atlantic a few miles from New Bedford, Massachusetts, alongside a Russian trawler immediately after the bombing. A few hours before, the plane had been seen by the anti-Communist underground taking off from a field in Florida below the 26th parallel. Fishermen who witnessed the ditching of the B-24 got to the pilot before the boats from the Russian trawler, and rushed him to New Bedford. But UNIT had been tipped off and its agents were at the beach when they landed. The captive was taken from the fishermen and whisked off to a Naval Hospital. The pilot was not Cuban but Chinese. The Communications Workers Union went on strike to tie up the telephone lines, but they were too late. Huckins' telephone grapevine had gone into high gear and the word got out.

Once the truth was known, the cover-up started immediately. President Gunther petitioned the UN to investigate "in order to avoid an international ball of fire that would consume civilization." He suggested that Nu Phong, Chief Justice of the World Court head "a Commission of Champions in the pursuit of peace."

The United Nations ordered all NATO, SWAPO and SEAPO forces on full alert, but no aircraft or fleet units were allowed to leave their bases until the "Commission of Champions" could make its report. All attack units were ordered denuclearized in order to prevent "another terrible accident like the Boston tragedy."

Everyone knew that all Cuban and Chinese atomic weapons were controlled strictly by the Russians. The bombing an accident? How was that possible? Yet the Commission hammered away about "world hysteria" and provocative right-wing statements that had snapped the mind of a psychotic pilot." But their psychotic pilot was never produced. He committed suicide, UNIT said. No one really believed this. It was generally assumed that UNIT was an arm of the Russian secret police.

Later, the Chinese pilot was to be seen walking the streets of Prague signing autographs -- a true hero of the Soviet Union.

Weeks and months passed but the "Commission of Champions" made no report. Soon, mention of Boston disappeared from the pages of the newspapers as completely as Boston had disappeared from the face of the earth. No report was ever made. Moscow, Peking and Havana *remained intact*.

15. Mary Swain

Mr. and Mrs. Harvey Swain and their 19-year-old daughter Mary sat down to dinner in their Hartford, Connecticut, home. Mary had just arrived home from college for the holidays and the foot-high blanket of snow guaranteed a white Christmas. Mary was studying at one of New England's best colleges for women, at great cost and sacrifice to her parents. To her high school-educated mother a degree from this particular college represented about the highest achievement attainable.

"Wasn't that awful about Professor Glenn asking the President to give Puerto Rico to Russia in exchange for the Kamchatka Peninsula?" Mrs. Swain chattered on without pause. "Of course, I'd never *heard* of Kamchatka before I read about it in Glimpse but can you imagine such a crazy thing -- and from a professor right at your college!"

Mary sliced her roast beef slowly and bit her lip as she waited for her mother to run down. Finally unable to stand it any longer, she interrupted. "Well, Mother, Professor Glenn says that Kamchatka is an area of tremendous promise and it has as much coast line as our entire Eastern Seaboard. So it seems to me it's more~ than a fair trade. You should study history more, Mother. Doctor Glenn says that Kamchatka was discovered in the sixteen hundreds. This is the same era as the Spanish exploration of Puerto Rico and the rest of the Caribbean. Don't you see the tie-in and the psychological impact that this territorial exchange would have on world opinion?"

Knowing that she could not compete with her daughter on this plane, Mrs. Swain grew restive. Mr. Swain ate slowly and listened in silence. "Well, I don't know anything about psychology," Mrs. Swain replied weakly, "but I think the whole thing is silly."

"Well, Mother, it's *not* silly," Mary replied tartly. "Puerto Rico is just 5,000 square miles of real estate. Kamchatka is *sixteen times* that size. And besides, what has Puerto Rico got but a lot of rum, coconuts and fat, retired millionaires?"

Her father started at this. He had begun noticing peculiar and disturbing changes in his lovely daughter. She had never been opinionated or disdainful toward others, and politics had been beyond her purview. Eighteen months at that fancy college had changed all that, he concluded glumly. Her warmth was gone; she now considered it too maudlin to kiss him on the cheek when greeting him.

Mary had always been sensitive and prone to take herself too seriously. In high school, she had been beset with doubts about man's purpose on earth. Why did she exist? Was there a God who cared? Was there a God at all? She went to Reverend Peake, their family minister, in a state of extreme depression, looking for answers; looking for bedrock upon which to build her life. The Reverend Peake did not shore up her already weak and crumbling foundations -- a porous foundation containing many locules of doubt, and high school-engendered bewilderment.

The Reverend Doctor Peake was of the new school of religion. He sounded more like a psychiatrist than a minister. Psychiatry and metaphysical philosophy had largely replaced theology in Christian ministerial training. What theology they taught was comparative, eclectic; impartial between Buddhism, Christianity, Hinduism and the others. Science and reason had replaced them -- and psychiatry rose like a phoenix from these philosophical and theological ashes to preside over man's inner needs.

The Reverend Doctor Peake explained to Mary that her basic problem was sexual guilt and that she should release these unhealthy inhibitions. These unreleased sexual urges, he explained, caused pimples, headaches and menstrual irregularity. The Reverend Peake had always been fascinated by Mary's peaches and cream complexion, voluptuous body and long auburn hair. Sensing an opportunity he had long yearned for, Peake screwed up his courage and made his bid. He walked around his desk and stood very close to Mary's chair. With a trembling hand on her head he had suggested in as kindly and warm a voice as he could muster that he was well enough experienced and sufficiently understanding to help her over "the delicate initial love experience." Mary, shocked, horrified and completely unprepared for such a proposal, bolted from his office in tears. She never went to church again.

Mary had ceased dating when home on vacation and spent most of her time in her room reading and making notes. Her naive and unsuspecting mother had interpreted this to mean that she was going steady with someone at college. Mary had neither confirmed nor denied this.

Mary was "going steady" but it was with an ideology as well as with a man. She was the prettiest girl in her college class and Professor Robert Glenn lost no time in bringing her under his intellectual aegis. Professor Glenn, young, arrogant, brilliant, had shown Mary a new world in the making: a perfectly ordered world where no one was allowed to be unhappy. If there was a heaven, Glenn said, we had to make it here on this earth. And Communism was God's answer, if there was a God, to heaven on earth. The sexual climax, he told her, was the only moment of truth he had ever seen and the only one he ever expected to see. He suggested to Mary that they seek as much "truth" together as possible.

Mary needed little convincing -- Reverend Peake, although he failed in his attempt at seduction, had prepared the way.

Her family had attended well to Mary's temporal needs; her clothes, her education in the arts and sciences. But they had neglected the spiritual core, having left that to a church that, unrecognized by them, no longer dealt with the spirit. This highly sensitive and beautiful young woman, looking for a purpose in life, was ideal material for the brain-twisters and soul-scorchers such as the Peakes and the Glenns of church and campus.

Mary's nimble mind, with Glenn's help, had quickly absorbed everything to which it was exposed. It was first exposed to small but constant doses of socialism in the guise of "human welfare" and then to Marxism in the guise of "environmental psychology." With her eager mind thus prepared, hatred and contempt for America quickly came to fruition through distortion of American history, ridicule of America's religious heritage and the teaching of perverted economics.

By the time her family had paid the last of her tuition, Mary was a confirmed Communist, completely stripped of all moral principle and devoid of any compassion for man -- except when taken as an omelet. The single eggs did not count. She was willing to break her share, to make that beautiful omelet -- the world socialist order: one government, one police force in a world free of war. The only monopoly, Mary reasoned, would be the government which would parcel out equal shares to all, no matter what their station in life. Their place in the social order was all due to environment anyway. Why should a scientist get more than a barber just because his exposure to intellectual ferment had been greater? Mary Swain and Yuri Rudenko, alias Seneca, were different breeds of the same species. Mary really believed the Communist dialectic with all her heart. Yuri, having seen it in action, could take a choice: revulsion and escape, or acceptance of the horror and cooperation with it. Mary had never been confronted with this choice.

After graduation Mary went to New York City for graduate work in psychology. The university work was merely a cover so that she could continue her activities with the Communist Party. Sympathetic faculty superiors saw to it that she had little to do, thus freeing her for organizational duties and training in espionage and subversion.

During the next seven years Mary was tested and retested. She was not only tested for loyalty but for her ability to withstand boredom, to take and carry out the most outrageous orders and to submit to any humiliation for The Cause. Because of her beauty and cleverness Mary was most useful for compromising important people and this became her forte.

Mary Swain was used as a "sleeper"; a dedicated agent who is dropped into a community to become a respected part of that community and to remain dormant, like the tubercle bacillus, until the proper conditions present themselves. When the conditions are right and the order is given, the virulent organism turns on a target organ within the body politic upon which it has fed -- and usually fed very well. Mary Swain, a highly unlikely-looking Communist agent, was the invading bacterium. Dr. Dwight Huckins, after his exposure of the Boston plot, was selected to be her next target organ. Huckins, with his infernal telephones, had scotched too many of their plans. He had to be destroyed.

The Communists had tried everything to discredit Dr. Huckins. Communist lawyers, through contacts in the hospital, watched his every move on every case. Periodically, malpractice suits would be filed against him. The newspapers and the legion of whisperers would see to it that the populace heard of the suit but not the vindication. The publicity was devastating. They tried to undermine his credit, his employees and his family.

The whispering campaigns were unremitting, clever and vicious. Any female patient or friend under sixty years of age would be mortified by a telephone call to her husband: "You know, Mr. Robbins, your wife is seeing an awful lot of Dr. Huckins. Don't you owe it to yourself to find out why?"

Huckins was constantly whipsawed between friend and enemy. His friends urged him to "give up this obsession of yours" for the sake of the children. His enemies urged the same thing -- anonymously. He was called a Communist agent provocateur, a playboy, a quack, a Ku Kluxer, an alcoholic.

From across a neighborhood fence:

"Did those pills Dr. Huckins gave you help?"

"No, I'm seeing him again tomorrow."

"Well, dear, if you don't mind a little friendly advice, I'd change doctors. You know, he's mixed up with that awful Figueres woman and -- this is strictly confidential -- the FBI watches him *constantly*. No one seems to know exactly *what* he does but -- can you afford to be involved? I mean Dan being a vice president at the bank and all that --." Another seed was planted and eventually another patient lost. Finally, his practice was reduced to the hard core of his devoted followers. They could not be shaken loose because they believed in him. The attacks continued unremittingly and kept his practice from growing, but beyond this they could not hurt him further.

As his income contracted, the family would contract in its financial commitments -- with no complaint. They sold their summer cottage in North Carolina and cut back on household expenses. Martha worked weekends and after school and David's allowance was discontinued ... at David's suggestion. The family worked as a team; a team that sees its goals clearly: its own survival and the survival of the country that gave it birth.

Mary Swain came to Dr. Huckins as a patient in January, 1980, after the atomic bombing of Boston. The master plan called for her to ingratiate herself with him for a full year and then a frame-up was to be engineered. The Party supplied her with two young children -- her husband "had been killed in an automobile accident." She was also supplied with a liberal amount of money.

For one medical reason or another, Mary managed to see Dr. Huckins at least fort-nightly. If she had no legitimate ailment, some pretext concerning the children would be concocted. Dwight made a number of house calls on Mary Swain during the ensuing year. Movies of his entering and leaving were taken from a house across the street.

Mary was a dedicated Communist but she was also a woman. She had never met a man with Dwight's iron will and self-control. Her senses told her she excited him; yet she knew, almost from the beginning, that he would never make an improper advance. She feigned interest in his patriotic endeavor and, in spite of herself, had to admire him for his love of country and determination to save it from the Communist onslaught. He reminded her of her father who had ranted constantly about "Communist slavery." She had always had nothing but disdain for opinions like Dwight's and her father's, but Dwight was somehow different. He caused a warmth and churning within her that she had never experienced.

During the course of the year they had had a number of philosophical discussions in his office. Recognizing immediately her Marxist attitudes and lack of religious convictions, Dwight began to chip away at her philosophy almost from the very beginning. During one of their discussions the question of atheism among intellectuals came up and Mary challenged Dwight on the ground that most modern intellectuals did not agree with him. His reply, with its logic, changed the course of her life: "Do the modern day academicians preaching atheism have some insight that the great masters did not possess? If so, then let them produce something to equal Michelangelo's Pieta, El Greco's Golgotha or da Vinci's Last Supper. Don't you think it possible that these *proven geniuses* might possess some religious insight that the average mind does not? Isn't it the height of egotism for these campus prodigies to say, 'We know it all. God is dead.' How do *they* know?"

For weeks Mary pondered over this dialogue with Dwight. She knew that he was more intelligent than she, and he seemed so much more practical than the college professors that had formed her opinions. Could he be entirely wrong? Were the professors entirely right? Had she worked and sacrificed during the past eight years only to hurt or destroy people like Dwight Huckins?

On her last visit to his office, Dwight handed her a prescription across the desk.

"Take one of these four times a day. By the weekend your throat should be back to normal." He came around the desk and took Mary by both hands. "And don't worry about Tommy. He is about the trillionth kid to get measles and he'll be O.K. He seems awfully sick but a little tincture of time will cure that."

Obviously disturbed, she heard hardly a word.

"Mary, you seem awfully depressed today and I don't think you've heard a word I said. Is there something else?"

Mary blinked. "No, Doctor, everything is fine." Mary reached out impulsively and straightened Dwight's tie pin. "You look awfully tired," she said. "Are you getting enough sleep?"

Dwight was startled by the sudden intimacy. "Well, no, I guess not but most doctors don't, you know." During the awkward silence he studied her. Dwight realized more than did Mary, that she was starting to rebuild her faith and that he was, one at a time, supplying the building blocks.

Dwight turned back to his desk. "Mary --sit down a minute." He motioned her into a chair. "In my years of medical practice I have seen a lot of people go full circle from religious faith, to agnosticism, to atheism, back to agnosticism and then back to an unshakeable religious faith." Detecting that she was receptive to this personal turn in their discussion, he continued. "I have the feeling that you've passed the distal end of the circle's diameter and are returning to something that you need very much."

Tears welled up in her eyes. "If he only knew how rotten I am!" she thought. Mary shook her head and carefully folded the prescription. "I -- I don't know, Dr. Huckins. I don't know what I believe any more. I wish I could see you more often -- to talk to you." She noted a flush to his face and quickly changed the subject. "Should I renew Tommy's cough medicine -- it's almost gone.

Dwight, on firmer ground, replied quickly: "Yes, and take his temperature in the evening. It's more likely to be elevated then."

"Thank you. I will." Her large gray eyes met his briefly. Dwight was relieved when the door closed behind her.

Mary drove home slowly, fighting back the tears. Finally, unable to control herself, she stopped by the road and wept openly. She was caught in her own web. The course was set and her superior would brook no deviation from that course. "History must continue its inevitable unfolding," Professor Glenn had said. Many good people would have to be sacrificed in the making of a world free of capitalistic oppressors. Mary Swain would have to destroy the only man she had known in her 30 years whom she really loved.

* * *

The plot was carefully planned and put into operation on a Friday afternoon. Movie cameras, a tape recorder and infrared light for photography in the dark were set up in Mary's bedroom. The office telephone rang late that Friday and the secretary called Dr. Huckins on the intercom. "It's Mary Swain, Doctor -- she sounds awfully sick."

Dwight picked up the receiver. "Yes, Mary."

"Doctor, I'm terribly sorry to bother you so soon again but I thought this might be important."

"What's up, Mary?"

"Well, I've been vomiting since this morning and I have an awful pain around my navel -- could it be appendicitis 7'

"Yes, it could be. I'll be through here in 20 minutes and I'll drop by on the way home. You can put an ice bag on your stomach but don't take any medicine." Dr. Huckins buzzed the secretary on the intercom. "Evy put Mary Swain on my house call list, please."

Bone-tired and hungry, Dr. Huckins left the office at six and headed east toward Mary Swain's house. He checked in with the answering service on his radio-telephone. "Seven-five-nine reporting on station. Will you call my wife please and tell her I'll be late for dinner?"

"Ten-four, Doctor. We have no further calls for you at this time."

Mary stood by the telephone extension in the living room of her home in a gossamer negligee. Her moment of truth -- as Dwight would define it rather than Glenn -- was at hand. Three of the "monsters" (as she had come to call them) had, for all intents and purposes, taken possession of her home. Dwight would arrive in a moment and then that precious person would be destroyed. He would be driven from the city in disgrace; his life, his home, his cause -- sullied and discredited. And she would then move on to smash the life of another dedicated patriot. Who would it be next time? A minister? A business man? Some poor mechanic in a vital defense industry with greasy hands and a heart full of love for his God and his country?

She watched the three party-disciplined brutes through the bedroom door as they moved about making their final preparations. They pulled the blinds, rechecked their infrared lights and then one of them brusquely motioned for her to come into the bedroom.

What would they do to Dwight? Would they attack him or would they rely on her to entice him into her bed? She knew that this would be impossible but she had not told them. They would have to smash his wonderful brain into unconsciousness. They must be stopped -- Dwight must be warned!

The biggest one, the one with the lethal-looking switch-blade knife, motioned to her. "Come on, Sis, get your butt in here -- do you wanna mess up the whole thing?" he snarled.

Mary's hand was on the phone. Her heart pounding, she stood stiff and pale. Her febrile mind raced. There wasn't time to call Dwight. They would kill her before she got to him. There was one hope: dial the operator and pray that the message got through.

Her trembling hand picked up the phone and she dialed "0." "Operator," she whispered, "this is important -- call the Doctors' Answering Service. Tell them to tell Dr. Huckins not to come -- the pain is gone now."

And the pain was indeed gone as the burly one, realizing that she had thwarted their carefully laid plan, leaped across the room with a growl and plunged his knife into her neck. Blood gushed from the wound. Mary collapsed silently to the floor.

They dragged her bleeding body onto the bed and placed the knife in her right hand. Quickly gathering their equipment, they bolted out the back entrance.

* * *

Dr. Huckins' convertible had covered half the distance to the Swain house when his car telephone buzzed. "Seven-five-nine. Come in please."

Dwight picked up his microphone. "This is seven-five-nine. Go ahead."

"Doctor, we had a rather peculiar message. That Mrs. Swain just called back through the telephone company operator and told her to tell your answering service that the pain was gone and she didn't want you to come. The operator said she sounded strange and whispered the message."

"Ten-four. Thank you." Dwight felt intuitively that something was terribly wrong. Increasing his speed, he decided to go to Mary in spite of her cryptic admonition.

Dwight pressed Mary's front doorbell. There was no response. He entered without further ringing, feeling a vague foreboding. The living room was empty and silent. "Mary, it's Dr. Huckins." Walking to the bedroom, he noticed the blood-spattered telephone and the pool of blood on the living room rug.

Mary Swain lay on her bed, the knife in her right hand. Blood half covered her body. To the doctor's experienced eye the situation was obviously hopeless and resuscitation impossible. Trying to remain detached, he calmly picked up the bedside telephone to make the necessary calls. It was then he noticed the handwritten note hidden under the telephone and dated the day before:

"Everyone should have someone or something to die for. I have found my someone."

16. The Drunk

(EASTER, 1981)

When the Communist conspiracy sets out to liquidate an enemy, little is left to chance. If one plan fails, another is ready for implementation. No cost is too great. No amount of planning, time, effort, scheming and subterfuge is considered excessive. Once a liquidation is deemed necessary, the victim is among the living dead. The order for liquidation and the act itself are virtually identical, the difference being only a temporal thing -- and Communists have a lot of time and patience.

The house call seemed routine. The telephone jangled next to Dwight's head at three o'clock in the morning. He swung his legs out of bed before picking up the receiver. Huckins had learned from long experience that he was less likely to go back to sleep after making a commitment if he answered the telephone in a sitting position, with both feet on the floor.

The voice at the other end sounded desperate. "Doctor, please come right away. I think my wife has had a heart attack."

He wrote down the address on his bedside pad. Near the airport, he calculated; a long way from home and, in that area, probably a charity case. He always felt irritated and put upon by these night calls that usually turned out to be unnecessary but he never failed to go.

Dwight slipped into his clothes, yawned, picked up his black bag and reached for the light switch. Beth always scolded him the next day if he left the bedroom light on. Then he remembered, the last fog of sleep having cleared, that Beth and the children were not there. They were in Hartford with the grandparents for the Easter holidays.

The air was sweet and clean. As he left the house he was greeted by his favorite sounds: the soft rattle of wind through coconut fronds and the distant lap of the surf. How could anything be wrong with the world on a night like this? Dwight inhaled deeply. His love affair with the Gulf of Mexico was eternal and deeply pleasurable.

His heart was still heavy with the tragedy of Mary Swain. Why had she done such a hideous thing? Who was this "someone" who drove this exquisite and thoroughly sweet creature to self-destruction? Mary had always confided in him ... why hadn't she told him?

Or was it really suicide? Could she have cut her throat that deeply, severing the carotid artery and the jugular vein, and then gotten into a bed fifteen feet away in another room? This would be impossible in a state of hemorragic shock. Would she still have the knife in her hand? Unlikely.

The note appeared to have been written by Mary. It must have been written in advance as the date indicated, he reasoned, and secreted under the telephone. If so, then she must have known that her life was in danger. But why? Was this "someone" a new bye interest resulting in the spurning of another who then threatened to kill her?

When the sheriff arrived, Dwight recalled that he blurted out: "This is no suicide. *This is murder!"*

But when Dwight queried him later, he claimed to have made a hasty judgment and had now changed his mind. The coroner signed out the case as suicide and the District Attorney refused to discuss it. There appeared to be unseen political factors at work but with Mary Swain, Dwight reasoned, that just didn't make any sense.

He felt unexpected pangs of jealousy toward this unknown man. Dwight was realistic enough to recognize the attraction that he had felt for her and she for him. But he was mature enough to know that surrender to her would have only lead to a string of disasters for his beloved wife and children and probably for Mary as well. But perhaps, he mused, if he had been a little closer to her he could have prevented her suicide--or her murder. The truth about Mary

Swain would have both shocked and hurt him. Mary knew this, and by her sacrifice she had obviated this possibility forever.

He drove out of the driveway, around the sharp bend in the secondary road and onto the highway leading to the city. "It'll be about 20 minutes both ways this time of night," he thought. "I should be home by 4:30." He wound his watch then flipped the switch turning on his radio-telephone. "This is seven-five-nine, reporting on station. I'm on a house call to the airport area... over." No answer. "The damned thing's on the blink again," he fumed.

The small white frame house (vintage 1930) was set on concrete blocks. In the moonlight Dwight could see automobile parts and assorted junk strewn around the weed-filled yard. A dim yellow light emanated through the screen door. Dwight knocked.

"Dr. Huckins?" someone asked behind him. "Yes, is this... " There was a sudden ringing in his head and jabbing pain in his left shoulder. In a state of semi-consciousness Dwight was aware of voices and the shuffling of feet. Then he felt a sharp pain in the back of his throat. Dwight's medically trained brain began to panic ... something terrible was being done to him! He flailed desperately with both arms and legs. His head was held fast and something was being stuck up his nose. The sharp pain returned to his throat; he vomited and then choked on it. A voice snarled, "Slug him again." Dwight Huckins lost consciousness.

* * *

"Dr. Huckins is in no condition to be examined now..."

Dr. Tom Mahan cut in, "Dr. Apfel, Dwight is my best friend. I have every right to see him not only as his friend, but as his physician. What right have you to tell me that Dwight can't be examined when he specifically asked for my consultation?" Dr. Mahan had never talked to a colleague bike this but he was furious. Also, he knew that he was on good legal and ethical ground.

Dwight had been picked up by the police. He was found lying on the front floor of his car with an empty whiskey bottle beside him. The car was in a ditch. Dr. Herman Apfel, Chief of Psychiatry at Sarasota General, had arrived at the police department soon after Huckins was brought in. Apfel claimed that someone in the police department had called him to see Dr. Huckins. He had diagnosed Huckins as having delirium tremens and had had him admitted immediately to the psychiatric ward of Sarasota General Hospital.

Although Tom Mahan was an ear, nose and throat specialist he knew, as every physician does, that delirium tremens is the result of years of heavy drinking and poor dietary habits. He knew -- and he knew that Apfel knew -- that Dwight Huckins was not a drunkard..

"Are you going to let me in or do I go to the Chief of Staff?"

Dr. Apfel feigned indifference, ignored Tom's question and called an orderly. "Take Dr. Mahan to see Huckins -- Room 502," Apfel said in his heavy Viennese accent.

"I want to see Dr. Huckins alone," Tom demanded.

"Help yourself," Apfel wheeled and walked toward his office. His neck was blue-red, the veins distended, giving away his suppressed rage.

Tom looked after him. "I hope he has a stroke," he muttered between his teeth.

The young Negro orderly seemed bored and uninterested. He preceded Dr. Mahan down the shining linoleum hail, unlocked a door and ushered him in.

"Leave the door open," Mahan ordered. The orderly shrugged, jammed the ring of keys into his pocket and started back down the hail. "With the door open he's your responsibility, not mine. He's gone 'skitzie,' so good luck."

Tom rushed into the room, fear cutting his breath short. Dwight Huckins a schizophrenic? . . . Impossible! The bare room reeked of alcohol. Dwight was lying on his back. His arms and legs were restrained by cloth binders that attached under the bed. Dr. Mahan's trained eye quickly summed up the physical findings: a two-day beard; bloodshot eyes; a tremor of the hands; dehydration; a very rapid pulse. It looked like a classical case of acute alcoholism with the D.T.'s. But, this was Dwight Huckins, M.D. What had they done to him? Why had Dwight, in a brief moment of lucidity, requested a nose and throat examination? Was he merely trying to alert a trusted friend or was there more to it than that?

There was no recognition in Dwight's eyes. Then he appeared to see something in the corner of the room. "Isn't it exquisite?", he exclaimed. Dwight raised his head and began to tremble. "My God, the colors!" His eyes glistened as if seeing a divine revelation. Rapturously he stared at the corner, transfixed. "Oh, oh, how lovely."

Dr. Mahan held his friend's shoulder. He was chilled and hypnotized by the intensity of Dwight's hallucinations. What on earth had happened? Being an ear, nose and throat specialist, Tom was on unfamiliar ground but he knew his basic clinical medicine. Dwight was not a heavy drinker and one bout of heavy drinking by a non-habitué' would not be likely to cause hallucinations. Tom's analytical mind began to pick up momentum. "And what about these beautiful 'things' Dwight is seeing? The hallucinations of alcoholism are things of horror and revulsion; snakes coming from the eyes and mouth, bugs on the skin -- rats and lizards." Tom's mind was racing now.

He took the nasopharyngoscope from his bag and gently inserted the thin instrument with its bright light on the tip into Dwight's nose. Dwight, now staring rapturously at the ceiling, ignored him. Through the instrument Tom could see that the posterior naso-pharynx was excoriated and bleeding. The puzzle was taking form. "They must have *tube-fed* him that whiskey!" he whispered aloud. He removed the bloody scope, wrapped it in a paper towel and dropped it into his bag.

He stared at Dwight as though expecting the answer to appear on his face. For the first time, he became aware of the faint odor of raw fish on Dwight's breath. The last piece of the puzzle fell into place. Only one drug in the world smelled bike that ... *silocorbin!* They had induced a state of psychosis in Dwight by giving him this terrible drug.

Tom remembered Dwight's quoting to him from Beria of the Russian Secret Police:

"You can cripple the efficiency of leaders by sticking insanity into them through the use of drugs. You can wipe them away with testimony as to their insanity." Dwight had pointed out that while under the influence of a schizophrenogenic drug such as silocorbin, a Red agent with the medical privileges of a psychiatrist could destroy the "patient" in a way far more terrible than murder: he could destroy him *by murdering the civilized portion of his brain* -- the frontal lobes. The frontal brain area can be destroyed by difficult-to-detect methods such as high frequency sound waves, shock therapy or by the use of an ice pick-like instrument inserted under an eyelid and into the brain through the skull, which is very thin in that area. When the frontal lobe is destroyed the victim becomes sloppy in dress, vile of tongue, and irresponsible in behavior. He may make sexual advances in public; he may take a world cruise leaving his family and business affairs in utter chaos and ruin. If a man was once seen as an incompetent and fool, who would ever believe him again? Who would question his continued incarceration? Shouldn't the community be protected from such a person? Shouldn't he be protected from *himself?*

Tom examined Dwight's eyes carefully. There was no evidence of penetration under the bids. He flipped through the chart to the doctor's order page. "EST in AM -- Apfel." It was dated today which meant that he was in time to save Dwight from shock treatment.

Dr. Mahan now fully realized the enormity of the situation. The morning newspapers had had a field day: "Drunk and disorderly", "... exhibiting bizarre behavior", "...had been rumored for many months that Dr. Huckins was acting strangely." And on the editorial page: "Dr. Dwight Huckins, an outspoken opponent of the Mental Health Program, which he has labeled 'subversive', appears to be a victim of his own shortsightedness." Dwight Huckins was to be completely discredited and railroaded to oblivion in one smooth operation.

Mahan knew that he must act quickly and boldly if his friend was to be saved. There was no court order holding Dwight there. He had checked that before coming. Until a court order was rendered, Apfel had no legal hold on

Dwight. He would demand Dwight's release, thought Mahan, but he immediately rejected that. It wouldn't make sense under the circumstances; Dwight *did* appear severely disturbed. Tom paced up and down the barren room. He must take Dwight out on some medical pretext. Apfel couldn't refuse that, even if he suspected a ruse.

Dr. Mahan stuck his head out of the door. "Orderly!" he shouted. The orderly appeared almost before his echo had died. "Tell Dr. Apfel that I must see him at once," Tom said with all the authority he could muster.

"He's not here," the orderly replied.

"Then by God find him!" Tom immediately shot back. Somewhat cowed, the orderly grumbled and went down the hall. Tom returned to the room, determined not to bet Dwight out of his sight.

In an indiscreetly short time, Dr. Apfel entered the room. He smiled benignly at Dr. Mahan, ignoring the babbling patient. "What can I do for you, Dr. Mahan?"

"I must take Dr. Huckins to my office for a proper examination," Tom said. "He has blood coming from his nose and I can't examine him properly in this light. I need suction, more instruments and I can't position him correctly here."

Apfel's bushy brows met at the midline. Excitement always accentuated his accent. "Dot iss eempossible. Dr. Huckins iss a very sick man."

Dr. Mahan straightened up. "Dr. Apfel, Dr. Huckins requested *me* as his physician. You have no right to hold him without a court order. I will take full responsibility." He turned to the orderly who was lounging against the door sill. "Get me a stretcher and call an ambulance to the emergency entrance." The orderly looked at Apfel who nodded for him to comply.

Mahan was relieved to see Bob Harper, his favorite driver, pull up to the emergency entrance. Tom got in the back of the ambulance with Dwight. Harper started the powerful engine and turned to face his occupants. "They said to your office. Right, Dr. Mahan?"

"Hell, no, Bob. Head for Tampa and don't turn off your siren!"

17. Recovery

"Your father's nuts!" Charbey Figgins, half again the size of 14-year-old David Huckins, sneered at him. The other boys snickered and waited. Trembling with rage, David struck at the pale, pimply face. Blood squirted from Charley's pudgy nose. "Owww," he yelled as David's other fist caught him full in the mouth. Now a dozen fists were striking him on the face and head, or so it seemed. David, sitting on Figgins' chest, could not stop. When Figgins began to scream and cry, the other boys pulled David off. None of the boys ever mentioned David's father again.

He arrived home shaken, but proud. He had defended his father well and he liked the feel of victory. Dr. Huckins was reading the evening paper when his disheveled son came in.

"What happened to your lip, Dave ?"

"Oh, I got it nicked in basketball practice. It's not bad."

Dwight took his son's face in his hands. Feigning great interest, he studied the small cut. "Well, bet's see now." Without taking his eyes from the wound, he asked, "Did you win?"

David, his face held rigid by his father, lifted his eyes toward him. "Sir?"

"I said, did you win?" He bet go of the boy's face.

David blushed and broke into a grin. "Yes, Dad, I won and he was bigger than me."

"Correction; he was bigger than I."

So the rumors were still circulating, Dwight thought. Undoubtedly some thoughtless kid had said something about his sanity. Maybe it was true -- maybe there were subtle changes in his personality that he could not recognize. But he must not show his anxiety before his adoring son. "Come on, big boy, let's make some chocolate sodas."

Dwight Huckins had lived with a gnawing fear since his recovery from the beating and hospital frame-up. Had any permanent brain damage been caused? Often the signs of deterioration from frontal lobe injury would not show for six months. The victim would never notice the changes in himself -- but his friends would. Beth seemed overly solicitous. She seemed to hesitate before answering the simplest questions, as if she were afraid of inadvertently revealing something she knew that he did not.

For the third time in six months, Dwight went to see Gregory Wallin, the neurologist, for an examination. "Lights out, Margaret." The nurse turned out the light and the blackened room was pierced by a thin rod of white light from Dr. Wallin's ophthalmoscope. He peered into Dr. Huckins' left eye. "No hemorrhages or exudates. The blood vessels are normal. Lights, please." The nurse turned on the bights and made some notes on a pad.

"O.K., Dwight, Stand up, put your feet together, your arms straight out and close your eyes." He observed for a moment. "Equilibrium is excellent -- cerebellar function normal. That will be all, Margaret. Put your shirt on, Dwight, and I'll see you in my office."

Dr. Wallin folded Dwight's chart, laid it on his desk and leaned back in his chair. Dwight, sitting across from him, stared intently at his colleague. "Dwight, it's been six months. I see absolutely no evidence of brain injury. Now, will you, once and for all, forget the whole thing?"

"Greg, nothing could make me happier. I'm convinced if you are." He tried to control the relief and exhilaration that he felt. Dwight Huckins was not afraid of death, but the fear of mental incompetence had left him inert and depressed. He sprang from his chair. "Well, Greg, I've got a lot of things to do." He stretched his hand out to his friend. "You've been swell about this. Thanks for your patience and understanding."

Dr. Wallin recognized the dramatic change in his patient. "Forget it, Dwight. Now get out of here and don't bother me any more."

As Dwight reached for the door handle, Dr. Wallin smiled and added, "It was ironic about Apfel, wasn't it?"

"Yes. He told everyone who would listen, including the newspapers, that I was an incurable schizophrenic. The day he went schizophrenic himself, I had been back to work a month. I was leaving the hospital as they put him in the ambulance. He took one look at me, turned as white as a sheet and screamed something about God having him by the throat."

"Do you think Apfel committed suicide?" asked Wallin.

"I don't know what to think, Greg. He could have hung himself but why those bruises on his head? They say he appeared to be living in mortal fear of something after I returned from Tampa. Everyone assumed that he was worried about the pending investigation of my case -- and he certainly had every reason to be. But frankly, I think whoever he was working with was afraid he would talk -- and liquidated him."

"Yes, I think you're right. I also think you're damned lucky to be alive and healthy after what you went through." Dr. Wallin offered his hand. "Give my regards to Beth, Dwight."

"Thank you, Greg. I will."

After leaving Greg Wallin's office, Dwight went to the nearest telephone and cabled home. "Hello, Beth. Greg Wallin said I'm healthy and am guaranteed not to get any stupider --how about dinner out tonight?" There was a long silence. "Hello, Beth -- are you there?"

"Yes, Dwight. I think we had better skip dinner out tonight. Can you come right home?"

"Yes, of course. What's up?"

"Tom is here," she answered pointedly. Dwight knew that something big must be brewing -- Mahan never came to the house during the day. For security reasons, they kept their public association strictly professional, and met for other purposes only at night. He sped home through a slashing rain.

18. Ratchet

Dwight cursed the deep holes in the high-way as he drove home through the rain. He thought back about the devastating deterioration that had taken place in the United States in the three years since his return from Washington. He had been aware of the deterioration long before, but in the last three years the decline had been precipitous.

The rain stopped but the gray-black clouds promised more. Dwight rolled down his window to smell the clean air. He turned the steering wheel back and forth to dodge the larger of the water-filled holes in the pavement. Before he went to Washington, the drive from the hospital to home, even during the heaviest of traffic, took only ten minutes. Now it took twenty-five. "The weed of socialism has certainly flowered in the soil of free enterprise," he reflected, "and that soil has become arid and non-productive.", Fewer and fewer people were making more and more decisions and, in the process, the rest of the people had forgotten how

to think, even how to maintain what they had --
the deteriorating roads being only one example.
Dwight compared this intellectual decline to that
of the Aegeans of ancient Crete who had forgotten how to read and write.

Gigantic athletic events provided by the
state now consumed most of the people's free
time. Meaningless political charades gave the
masses a feeling of participation in a government
they no longer understood or cared about. As long
as the entertainment continued and the food cou-
pons flowed unabated, the people asked no questions. Desecration of religious and other artistic
treasures was rampant. What had been beautiful
was now considered ugly and hateful. The grotesque had become exciting and "expressive of
man's release from the stultifying restraints of tradition." That is what the modern arbiters of cul-
ture said. In painting, primitive daubs were
acclaimed as "sensitive," deformed statuary was
said to show "great character and strength." Purile
literature, for those who could still read, was
widely feted. The filthier the language and the
more brazen the description of perverted acts,
the louder the acclamation and the higher the
award. This artistic degeneration reminded
Dwight of the Emperor Polybius observing Ro-
man soldiers playing dice on an exquisite Greek
painting which they had torn from the wall as if
it were a piece of common wallpaper.

Dwight had watched technological regres-
sion quickly follow the cultural decline. Grandi-

ose dreams of voyages to the moon were now forgotten as more mundane problems came to the fore and consumed the nation's time and energy. "The moon is a long way away," Dwight mused, "to a people who can't even keep their roads in shape." Maintenance of the highly developed urban civilization of the twentieth century was impossible with so few working so little.

With intellectual and economic stultification, missiles and other complicated weapons became too unreliable and dangerous to use. After hundreds of deaths from missiles turning back on their pads or landing in a neighboring town, the public outcry grew so loud that the entire program was finally abandoned. The missiles, now rusting on their pads, stood as monuments to the scientific genius of the past -- and the slovenliness of the present. The atomic bombing of Boston had been the last gasp of modern warfare. In later crises, atomic bombs were dropped but none of them had detonated. Such technological decline worked in favor of those nations having the largest tonnage of human flesh to throw at the enemy. The effect of this power shift had been portended in the invasion of Hawaii in 1978. Without the support of tanks or air cover, using the simplest bolt-action rifles with bayonets attached, hordes of Chinese had overwhelmed General Trotter's small garrison at Pearl Harbor and killed every one of Caucasian descent not evacuated by Trotter.

Dwight recalled bitterly how he had tried to warn people with influence, from the President down, about the general decline and especially about the enervation of America's defense posture. But few listened and even fewer comprehended. He had urged that every able-bodied man, woman and older child in Hawaii, and the other States as well, should be armed with a good rifle and know how to use it. But private weapons had long since been outlawed and seized by the government purportedly to "prevent crime."

In reply to his letters, the Peace Department had said, "General Wade Hampton Trotter, an experienced and capable commander, assures us that he anticipates no trouble in his area." Dwight knew enough of Trotter's reputation to realize that this was a lie and Trotter had later confirmed this at a press conference.

When the Hawaiian invasion came, only the criminal element and the Communists had arms; the general population was helpless. But Dwight had been gratified to see one good come from the Hawaiian tragedy. The people of the other forty-nine States, ignoring the gun registration laws, began quietly to arm themselves.

Dwight arrived home to find Dr. Mahan pacing the living room. The Gulf was gray, tumultous and foamy. Dirty white clouds drained the sunset of its color. The sun settled unnoticed; day turned to night without warning.

Beth turned on the living room lamps. In the nearness of the light, Tom Mahan looked pale and exhausted. He was wearing a dripping raincoat and Dwight noticed the 45-calibre automatic pistol in his belt. Flashes of light bounced from his rimless glasses as he turned and paced.

"Huck, I'm afraid this is it."

Tom related that UN troops under the command of General Kenyomo Gabonga had crossed the 26th parallel and were entering the outskirts of Ft. Myers, ninety miles south of Sarasota. Race riots had erupted all over that city.

"You know what it means, Huck," Tom said. "They're only ninety miles away and I doubt if they'll even slow down on their way here." Beth, pale and motionless, sat on the sofa.

Dwight took off his raincoat and sat down beside her. He was calm and composed. This news was expected. It had been only a matter of time. A mountain of propaganda on television, radio and in newspapers had been directed against Florida's west coast recently. A Sunday feature article the week before was headlined, "Pockets of Narrow-minded Nationalism Hurt Unity and Threaten the Peace." The article listed areas, among them the west coast of Florida, where "nationalist and segregationist fanatics are causing disunity and hindering the fight against Communism."

It was obvious to the Underground that the UN was planning another of its ratchet maneuvers. Because the local police forces were loyal to their local communities and could not be depended upon to help enslave their fellow citizens, they had to be neutralized or subdued on some pretext. The UN, in cooperation with the nation's press, usually performed its ratchet maneuver against the local authorities with deadly precision.

The ratchet technique consisted of a carefully planned series of "racial uprisings." The local police were overpowered and UN troops, all foreign, moved in "to establish law and order." All police and known anti-Communists were tortured and killed. The women were "used for the health of the army." The wheel turned and the ratchet clanked forward another notch. Concurrently, rioting would start in an adjoining city. With cries of "Freedom Now!" from Communist insurrectionists, the police department would be stormed and the UN forces would prepare another "liberation." The ratchet would move another notch forward.

With the first turn of the ratchet, the Florida West Coast operation started in Ft. Myers, just north of the 26th parallel. Communist operatives wrecked and killed. The local police were overpowered and the President, with perfect timing, called for "UN assistance" for Ft. Myers.

"Ft. Myers is hopeless," Tom said. "It came too fast. General Trotter thinks we should make our stand here. We are setting up a barricade at the intersection of Stickney Point Road and U.S. Route 41. Their tanks will have to traverse that route. 11' things go true to form, the local Reds here will attack the police department and the power plant. They'll probably start raising hell any moment and we're going to have a nice surprise ready for them."

Tom explained Dwight's job. He was to cruise between the power plant on the north side of town and the police station on the east. Using his automobile telephone, he would keep Tom apprised of events and they could concentrate their people where needed most. "We have patrols with shotguns all over the city to stop telephone line cutters and looters -- and," Tom added, "they have been instructed to take no prisoners."

Dwight went to the bedroom and returned with a 30-calibre rifle and a small pistol. He handed the pistol to Beth. "You'd better get Marty and Dave home, Beth. The Everglades are wet this time of year so take the large survival kit."

Beth took the revolver. Her face was white and determined. "I'll take the children, Dwight, but then I'm coming back. You'll need all the nurses you can get." They looked at each other and were afraid to speak further for fear of giving away what they both already knew. Life had taken another turn and things would probably never be the same again. Suddenly they embraced and their thoughts were one. "The good life is; behind us; grab this moment; don't let it go -- stop time; try to turn it back; bring back the sun -- and the sail."

Mahan chambered his 45-calibre automatic, set the safety and shoved it back into his belt.

"We'll smash the local scum as soon as they make their move. Be ready at a moment's notice to move all units south to the barricade." Then he realized that he was not being heard. Touched, and slightly embarrassed by his own intrusion, he turned and looked toward the gray-white Gulf and the leaden sky.

Beth and the children, long since prepared for this emergency, left the house in twenty minutes. An alternate plan of flying them to Montana, where a secret camp had been established for women and children, had to be abandoned because of the lack of private aircraft. All private aircraft were in service reconnoitering UN troop movements. Although not as isolated as the Montana camp and therefore not as safe, the Everglades camp was well maintained, camouflaged and carefully guarded.

David had urged his father to allow him to stay and fight, in the event that Sarasota was ever attacked. But Dwight had convinced him that patrolling the children's camp was equally as important. Martha was to help care for the young and act as a courier when needed.

Beth, Martha and David headed due east on Stickney Point Road toward Arcadia in the family station wagon. Crossing U.S. 41, they saw frantic preparations being made to meet the impending UN onslaught. Men were working feverishly with trip hammers, picks and shovels digging stand-up trenches across the highway in front of the barricade. The huge barricade astride the four-lane U.S. 41 was made of old cars, cement bags and an assortment of lumber, bricks, refrigerators, gravel and torn down street signs. The road east to the town of Arcadia, midway between Sarasota and the Everglades hideout, was heavy with traffic moving in both directions. Heading west toward Sarasota, the cars and trucks were loaded with men carrying rifles and equipment. The procession east was composed mainly of family cars loaded with children and groceries.

According to Air Reconnaissance, the route to Arcadia and thence southeast to the camp was free of enemy troops. Only one major north-south highway crossed their route to the camp and it was also barricaded to the south near the 26th parallel. Unless the UN Army made a sudden shift to the east in a flanking maneuver, it would be no threat to the fleeing families.

Beth, Martha and David, sitting together on the front seat, made the trip to Arcadia in complete silence. Occasionally, a small airplane would roar overhead, very close to the ground, barely clearing the tops of the automobiles. There were many of these small, private aircraft heading either toward or away from the 26th parallel. "It's comforting," Beth thought, "knowing that we at least control the air." Underground operatives within the UN Army itself had so effectively sabotaged the UN Air Force that the pilots had mutinied and had refused to fly the booby-trapped planes. Engines would quit on take-off; the planes would explode in the air or just fall apart with the first maneuver that caused more than average stress.

Dave and Marty knew that it was useless to ask their mother when she would return for them. Their father had not said goodbye. "Bring back some swamp cabbage," was all that he had said to Martha as he smiled and kissed her. He had handed the rifle to David and shook his hand, man to man. "Take care of Marty, Son. It's your job until we come for you."

David had gripped the rifle so tightly that his knuckles were white. The resolute jut of his jaw was almost an exact copy of his father's. "Don't worry, Dad. They may outnumber us but we're smarter than them."

"Correction, Son. We're smarter than *they*." They had looked at each other with a rapport that only a father and son could feel.

Beth and the children entered the Everglades camp at ten that evening. The water was high. Each mound of dry ground seemed to be floating like a giant mushroom in the tangled swamp. The grotesque and yet beautiful mangrove, like an endless serpent, moored the islands together. The occasional cry of a baby mingled with the constant belching of the frogs.

Groping through the darkness and wading through the knee-high water, they finally located the elderly Miss Walton, a retired school teacher upon whose thin shoulders the responsibility for the camp rested. Her tent was damp and the smell of bacon fat and smoke pervaded the air.

Beth wasted little time -- parting was easier that way. As soon as the car was unloaded she gave them each a silent farewell hug and headed back over the muddy road. Beth drove as fast as the deteriorated roads would permit. The car threw up mud on both sides like a snowplow as it cleaved its way back to Sarasota.

COTTON
GASOLINE

19. Molotov Cocktails

At the downtown Sarasota command post, teen-agers and oldsters, working against time and seldom looking up from their workbenches, filled pop bottles with gasoline and passed them down the assembly line to the next group where a small amount of detergent soap was added and each bottle sealed with a plastic top. At the last table in the line, a large ball of cotton was taped to the bottom of the bottle. The Molotov cocktails were then complete.

The command post and hide-out was located in an old commercial garage in the center of town, midway between the two most strategic points: the power plant on the north and the police station on the east. The building was barn-like with few windows. Those were covered with black cloth. The garage had been vacant for six months, but the original smell of grease, paint and gasoline lingered on. A typical garage calendar, with an overblown semi-nude at the top, hung over a scarred desk. Beth, on returning from the Everglades, set up her first aid station there.

Tom Mahan and Dwight met at the command post to give a final briefing to their inexperienced but determined little army. The depressing dampness combined with the dim light from undersized light bulbs would have been enough to dampen the ardor of most. But the courageous group listened intently, oblivious to their surroundings.

Dr. Mahan stood before a portable blackboard. "Picture yourself in an open field. You are being attacked by an enraged, red-eyed bull elephant. But this elephant is different: he is covered with steel armor plate and he's spitting hot lead in four directions at once. You have to experience a tank attack before you can appreciate it. Most people think of tanks as slow, lumbering, easy targets. But the tank, when attacking an objective such as our barricade, moves like an enraged elephant -- at 70 miles an hour."

Dismayed, everyone asked almost in unison, "Then how can we stop them?"

Dr. Mahan, having laid out the problem graphically and dramatically, continued. "The tank, like the elephant, has its vulnerable points. It has an optical system with which to see -- a periscope like a submarine. It has legs consisting of an endless tread. If you can knock out the periscope your monster is blind. If you can break one of his treads, your monster is crippled. And most important of all, the men inside the tank must have air to breathe. If you envelope the tank in flames, the men inside must escape -- or suffocate and roast. So it's not as bad as it at first seemed." There was some nervous laughter and shuffling of feet.

To the rear of the room, and casting a great bulky shadow over the gathering, was Reverend Bobby Tim Hadley. The Reverend Hadley, pink-cheeked and rotund, had straight black hair and pudgy hands. He was forty but looked thirty. His midwestern-accented religious Philippics had cracked and sizzled across the auditoriums of almost every city in the nation. He had stirred tens of thousands to action against the Communist infiltrators in the churches and the government. Because of his courageous exposures, he was an outlaw in the eyes of the government-controlled churches and the government itself. He was driven from radio by pressure being applied to the tightly regulated station owners. When President Silverbright was assassinated, the press tried to link this courageous man of God with the killing by implying that he had had a Rasputin-like influence over Carla Silverbright. He had visited the White House often but he had been there seeing his old friend Dwight Huckins; he had never even met the President's wife.

When the persecution became unbearable and agents of the United Nations Revenue Service began to snatch the collection plate right out from under his nose, he strapped two giant 45-calibre revolvers around his gigantic middle and offered his services as chaplain to the MacArthur Legion. His credo had always been simply, "Praise the Lord." Now it was, "Praise the Lord -- and pass the ammunition."

The Underground was basically a religious as well as a patriotic movement. They were fighting the anti-Christ, the anti-God. Against the forces of those who said, "There is *no* God," were arraigned the Christians, Jews and Mohammedans who said, "There *is* a God, whether he be called God, Yahweh, Jehovah, or Allah." The enlistment of Bobby Tim Hadley into the Underground gave it a religious cohesiveness and gave its members a constant reminder of why they were offering their lives, their fortunes and their sacred honor.

As Tom Mahan carefully explained the plan of battle, Bobby Tim stood like a large block of granite, awaiting his call. He would give them the word of God before they faced Him -- as some of them surely would before this day was done.

"When the tanks spot our barricade," Mahan continued, "they will charge full speed ahead to destroy it." Tom Mahan pointed to the diagram of their Stickney Point barricade chalked on the blackboard behind him. "The stand-up trenches we have placed across the highway, here and here, are about one hundred yards and fifty yards ahead of the barricade. These trenches will enable us to attack the tanks from the front, rear and sides. As a tank passes over the first trench we will hit him with these Molotov cocktails from the sides." He held up one of the gasoline-filled pop bottles with the large ball of cotton taped to the bottom. "When this breaks against the tank, the flaming cotton on the bottom will ignite the gasoline and, if enough of you hit it at once, will envelope the tank in flames and drive out the crew. If just one cocktail lands directly on top of the tank's turret, the flaming fuel will seep through the cracks and drive the crew out. So if your aim is good, one cocktail can often do the job very nicely. There will be a pan of gasoline in each trench. Wet the cotton with gasoline before igniting it. There is detergent mixed with the gasoline inside the bottle. It will stick to anything it touches and it's almost impossible to extinguish flaming detergent."

Someone in the back row spoke up. "What if we miss, Tom?"

"If you miss or the tank keeps coming anyway, those of us in the trench nearest the barricade will blast the engine in the rear with sticky grenades. If we fail, the third squad at the barricade itself will shove crowbars into the treads at the moment of impact. The tank will have slowed down enough to make this possible. The jammed tread will cripple the tank and then we'll hit him again with the cocktails. If that fails and a tank goes on into the barricade, the twenty-five pound land mines placed inside will detonate and automatically solve our problem. We'll have an enemy tank added to our fortification. And one more thing," Tom smiled and held up a little box, "don't forget your matches." There was another ripple of nervous laughter.

Tom paused and studied the faces before him. They were as ready as they would ever be to meet, head on, the awesome power of the United Nations. This was a group of desperate patriots, abandoned by their own government and being trapped as slaves of a world dictatorship. There was no choice but to resist. They knew only too well the stories of Katanga, Hungary and Miami. The horror of Ft. Myers was with them. They could only fight to set an example and hope for similar resistance with the next turn of the ratchet, wherever it might come.

If they could turn the enemy back, it would keep the resistance movement alive all over the country. If they could prove just once that the spirit of freedom still lived, the beautiful resort city of Sarasota would be remembered for a long time -- not just for its white beaches, but for the blood of its patriots.

Mahan glanced up at Bobby Tim standing in the rear of the room with a battered red leather Bible under his massive arm. Reverend Bobby Tim Hadley saw his mission clearly. This was no time for forensics. He knew that he was to deliver these children, right at this very moment, into the loving arms of God. The Word had to come straight and clear from his lips and into their hearts. He opened his Bible, paused and then read:

"Yea, though I walk through the valley of the shadow of death..." Some crossed themselves; others went to their knees. All activity in the garage ceased as Hadley's words, God's word, enveloped them. "...I will fear no evil: for Thou art with me; Thy rod and Thy staff they comfort me."

Tears came to Hadley's eyes and his voice rose to fairly shake the walls as he looked to the rafters and repeated the 24th Psalm: "This is the generation of them -- Oh Lord! -- that seek Thy face... The Lord strong and mighty, the Lord mighty in battle! Amen."

Fired with determination and an unshakeable faith, the group gathered up their equipment and dispersed to their assigned areas. In the bustle of the garage, Dwight caught a fleeting glimpse of Tokay Wren carrying a carton of Molotov cocktails out the back door. This was a different Tokay Wren. The superficiality was gone. Her lips were thinly drawn and there were telltale lines at the corners of her eyes from a sleepless night of gruelling work. Her satin black braid hung to the top of her tight denim dungarees. She looked darker, Dwight noticed -- and more beautiful than ever.

What a transformation takes place in people, he thought, when the fervor of patriotism flushes through them! A child becomes a man, sometimes overnight, when his sacred land faces critical assault.

A young couple in their late teens talked in a corner of the garage. The boy had a carbine slung over one shoulder. The girl, pale and tense, listened as he explained how to light and throw the gasoline bottles called Molotov cocktails. Satisfied that she understood, he put the bottle down and took both of her hands in his. They looked at each other for a moment and then parted; he to the south to harass the tanks and forward troops; she to the first trench with her crude weapons of war.

MIAMI
Ft. MYERS

20. Insurrection

The Communist uprisings in Ft. Myers had met no resistance by the underground. The first turn of the ratchet put the UN in control of Ft. Myers without firing a shot. Dwight listened to the distorted radio news reports as he drove between check points.

"This is Radio Station WUUN --A Special Bulletin." The announcer's voice was crisp and unemotional. "The UN Commander of SEAPO, the Southeastern Army Peace Organization, has announced that his troops, answering a plea for help from Ft. Myers, have occupied that beleaguered and strife-torn city. The commander, General Kenyomo Gabonga, stated this afternoon that the uprisings had been quelled and that all public facilities are under UN control. General Gabonga further stated that he hoped no further occupations would be necessary, but reports indicated that racial agitators were disrupting the city of

Sarasota to the north and his troops are
ready to aid that city if necessary. Stay
tuned for further developments."

Then followed a gay Latin rhythm. Dwight
turned it off. He recognized Gabonga's statement as a signal for the uprisings to start in
Sarasota and, almost simultaneously, heard the
crack of rifle fire in the direction of the courthouse. Putting the accelerator to the floor he
picked up the radio-telephone in his car. "This is
seven-five-nine. Call eight-one-three, please."
There was a pause. "Eight-one-three here --
over." Dwight inquired as to the situation at the
courthouse. "The courthouse and city jail are under attack. Our units are closing in on three
sides. The enemy has not gained access and
faces total annihilation."

Dwight smiled grimly. "Ten-four. Prepare
for immediate reassignment when your situation
is secured." He hung up and headed north along
the fashionable bay front. The street was de-
serted and the homes looked dark and timorous.
He turned onto Main Street and streaked toward
the power plant. A corpse pocked with gunshot
lay in the gutter in front of the jewelry store -- a
looter caught in the act.

As he turned onto North U.S. 41 near the
power plant it became obvious that the Communists had fared no better here. The road was
strewn with bodies. The underground was exult-
ant. Many, recognizing Dwight, held up their rifles and cheered as he passed.

Dr. Huckins picked up the telephone receiver and reported to Tom Mahan. "This is seven-five-nine. Give me Red Wing please."

Tom Mahan's voice boomed through. "Come in seven-five-nine."

"Tom, the power station and police headquarters remain secure. Enemy casualties were extremely heavy and ours appear minimal -- over."

"That's wonderful, Huck, but I'm afraid it's not going to stop the UN advance. I radioed SEAPO headquarters and told them the situation was well in hand here and that Sarasota needed no outside assistance, but they're pretending not to receive my message. I keep getting back crap like, 'Hold fast! Commander Gabonga has promised every assistance.' He'll 'assist' all right! I understand in Ft. Myers they're raping every female old enough to walk. They're burning men and boys alive after chopping off their privates --it's the Katanga massacre all over again."

Dwight, speechless with horror, had only one thought: Where was Beth? At last reports, she had been tending the wounded at the court house. His thoughts were interrupted. "Seven-five-nine, are you still there ?"

"Go ahead, Tom."

"Do you recall Mayor Small of Ft. Myers ?"

"Yes, he said we should collaborate with the Reds because survival was more important than freedom."

"Right. Well now he doesn't have survival or freedom. Ten of them made him watch while they raped his wife. Then they crucified them both by nailing them to his garage wall." The liberals never seem to learn, Dwight thought disgustedly. Cooperating with the conspiracy does not give them immunity; only the handful at the very center of the cabal avoid destruction -- and sometimes not even them.

Dwight's thoughts were suddenly interrupted by Mahan's transmission. "This is it, Dwight! Tanks are reported south of Venice coming hell-for-leather. General Trotter has promised help but they can't possibly get here in time -- it's some rifle unit out of Georgia -- get all squads to the barricade at once!"

"Ten-four, Red Wing, seven-five-nine out." Huckins U-turned with a screech of his tires and roared south back along the bayfront. He radioed all units to leave skeleton forces at key points and proceed immediately south to the Stickney Point barricade.

At dawn Gabonga struck. The sound of diesel motors and the creaking and clanking of heavy metal filled the air. Spotting the barricade, the first tank picked up speed and started blasting straight ahead with its cannon. As it passed over the first trench, the earth trembled, quake-like, from the blam-blam-blam of the tank's cannon. The young girl at the garage had obviously listened well. She lofted her flaming Molotov cocktail high into the air. It arced down and exploded squarely on the turret of the onrushing iron monster. The tank veered sharply to the right and the top hatch opened. Riflemen picked off the UN soldiers as they scrambled down from the tank, flapping at their flaming clothes.

The second tank, hard on the heels of the first, caught the advance trench unprepared. Tom Mahan, in the next trench, threw a "sticky grenade" against the rear of the tank as it roared over and away from him. The grenade stuck to the tank, exploded and tore away the engine and rear armor, revealing a bloody and smoking interior. The area quickly became a melee of smoke, flame, groaning injured, a constant blam-blam of cannon and a vicious whir of flying lead seeking a target of soft flesh.

Beth arrived at the fortification soon after Dwight and assisted him with the injured. Working silently together, they ignored the danger around them. Bobby Tim Hadley, standing like a massive oak, read from his battered Bible over the prostrate and pale body of a young man with a badly mangled arm. "The Lord liveth; and blessed..." A bullet passed through his left thigh, causing him to reel. "...be my rock; and let the God of my salvation be exalted..." A piece of shrapnel sliced across his right cheek. His right hand, clutching the Bible firmly, was soon covered with blood dripping from the wound on his face. The young man on the ground seemed to take new life as he observed the indomitable spirit of God's messenger. "He delivereth me from mine enemies: yea, Thou liftest me... Oh!" Bobby Tim went down with a tearing wound in the other leg. The boy, in spite of his shattered limb, rolled over onto his beloved chaplain to protect him from this rain of destruction -- and died there with a bullet through his head.

The next two tanks were also knocked out, but the fifth one drove straight through and slammed against the barricade. An old man shoved a crow bar into the track mechanism stopping the tank's forward motion. A desperate hail of machine-gun fire from the crippled tank sprayed in every direction in a last-ditch effort to hold off the dreaded flaming bottles.

From the left a large, bronze female form appeared through the smoke, leaped the barricade like a gazelle and charged the tank.

"Have a Coke!" she yelled as she tossed the flaming bottle. The tank's turret burst into flame and Tokay Wren fell with a hole in her chest that made sucking noises when she tried to breathe. Dwight quickly handed his morphine syringe to Beth and raced through the roaring heat to drag Tokay back behind the barricade. He covered her sucking chest wound with the cellophane from a cigarette wrapper. Beth handed him a large chest binder to secure the emergency dressing. Tokay was cyanotic but conscious. She spoke in short gasps. "Dr. Huckins -- I never -- told you -- the questions -- remember?"

"Yes, Tokay, I remember." There was a thin trickle of blood at the corner of her mouth. He called to a driver as he secured the dressing with a wide strip of tape: "Driver! Get this one to the hospital as quickly as you can and use nasal oxygen all the way in."

"My engine's overheated, Dr. Huckins -- I'm gonna have to stop for water."

"Never mind your water," he retorted. "Deliver these patients first and that's an order!" The young orderly snapped to and helped Dwight place Tokay's large, pain-wracked body in the ambulance alongside Hadley's. Bobby Tim would survive but Tokay had about one chance in twenty, he thought as he watched the ambulance, steam billowing from its radiator, careen around the bend in the road.

The blue-helmeted troops of General Gabonga's UN-SEAPO Command were not accustomed to fierce opposition. Home-grown traitors always did the dirty work for them, leaving it to the UN "peace forces" to move in and "rescue" the local populace. The sight of the flaming tanks threw the usually cocky troops into panic. Gabonga's flashy army quickly turned into a disorganized mob. Gabonga ordered the rear troops to shoot any man that retreated. But the howling, frightened soldiers up front, backtracking upon the rear guard, caused them to panic also. They dropped their rifles and stayed well ahead in the race back to Ft. Myers. The Underground, with captured tanks, decimated the UN ranks from the rear. It was said that General Gabonga, driving his own jeep, and alone, was the first to cross the Ft. Myers city line.

The victory was complete. Everyone knew the UN would think twice before trying any more "rescue missions's in the Sarasota area.

Beth left to bring the children back from the Everglades camp. While he waited for them Dwight, exhausted and covered with the blood of others, worked on doggedly to see the wounded off to the hospital.

Dwight had not had time to even think of the children until now. He had no way of knowing whether or not they had been overrun in a separate attack on the camp by Gabonga's uniformed cannibals. If this had occurred, Dwight knew that by now the camp would be a hideous and sanguinary abattoir. He had supplied Marty and David with cyanide capsules to be used in the event that capture became inevitable. Death would then be instantaneous and painless. Morose thoughts such as these gnawed at him as he worked and waited for three interminable hours.

Finishing a temporary leg cast on one of the remaining wounded, Dwight at last saw the family station wagon approaching from Stickney Point Road. He gave some final instructions to his aide and ran to meet the car at the barricade. He hugged David and Martha silently. Engulfed in the smell of gasoline fumes, and the stench of burned flesh, none of them spoke. They were all alive -- words could add nothing. As they drove away, the indefatigable Tom Mahan could be seen directing repairs and setting up patrols.

Dwight switched on the radio to see how the UNIFLIB propagandists would handle the underground's victory.

"...And now the latest WUUN news. From UN headquarters in New York: General Kenyomo Gabonga reports from the 26th parallel that stories of racial unrest in Sarasota were exaggerated. An on-the-scene inspection by General Gabonga revealed that local police forces have the situation well in hand. An interpreter, speaking for General Gabonga said, and we quote: 'No further rescue operations are anticipated in the Gulf Coast area.' Unquote. However, R. A. Seneca, UN advisor to President Gunther, has reported serious unrest throughout Area Four. He warned that more brushfire insurrections were possible, and even probable, as renegade General Wade Hampton Trotter, the Butcher of Waikiki Beach, continues to elude capture and lead the band of assassins and maniacs calling themselves the MacArthur Legion."

"In the areas of SEAPO, formerly called Florida and Georgia, the opportunistic bandits, masquerading under the false banner of patriotism, have become a real threat to peace and stability. President Gunther has announced that Mr. Samuel Yen, formerly with SWAPO in Texas and a dedicated international patriot, is to be sent into the troubled area to seek some solution to the problem."

The announcer became hysterical and dropped all pretense at impartial news reporting.

"The Underground is *powerful* and its agents are everywhere. None other than the Area Four Attorney General, Robbie Silverbright, the man whose job it is to know about subversives, has stated that the Underground has the power to strike down *anyone* when the time is right and the order is given.

"All of Area One is on the verge of collapse from the incessant and ubiquitous attacks of the so-called Free Europeans. Area Three is beleaguered by vermin calling themselves the Latin Legion. There are unconfirmed reports that the Formosans are at the outskirts of Peking. Inform your neighbors of the gravity of the situation. If they do not seem sympathetic -- inform on *them*. The front is everywhere and everyone must be prepared to sacrifice!

"Station WUUN in cooperation with UNIFLIB, your United Nations Free Flow of Information Bureau, has brought you highlights of todays news. Our next newscast will be at seven. Now back to Tune Time..."

David slapped his knee with delight. "Boy, we've really got them on the run, Dad!" David's enthusiasm was infectious and they all laughed at the obvious hysteria revealed by the radio announcer.

But Dwight knew that some sobering up of his family was going to be necessary. One battle did not make a war. He turned off the music, half-turned in his seat and slowed the car. "You know, we've had a victory but that doesn't mean we've won the war." He looked at their suddenly sobered faces and placed his hand on Beth's shoulder. "They're not going to lie down and play dead, you know.

"Do you think the broadcast is some sort of trap?" Beth asked.

"It could be. They might be planning to make an example of Sarasota. Our beach would make a perfect landing place for an amphibious attack."

They all paled at this thought. Dwight's predictions in the past had been uncannily accurate.

Martha enlarged on her father's prediction: "Maybe we'll *all* be back in the Everglades before long."

David caught the slight break in his sister's voice and moved quickly to shore her up. "Marty, how about a swim when we get home -- you can use my new snorkel." Martha grabbed his hand and squeezed it. Every girl, she thought, should have such a wonderful little brother.

Beth laid her head on Dwight's shoulder. He continued driving slowly, taking in the silence and brightness of the morning as contrasted with the hell of the battle behind them.

They crossed the one-lane bridge leading to the island and home. The bay shimmered like a million diamonds being shaken on a giant skillet.

Overhead, a perfect "V" formation of pelicans glided silently toward the Gulf.

About Doctor William Campbell Douglass II

Dr. Douglass reveals medical truths, and deceptions, often at risk of being labeled heretical. He is consumed by a passion for living a long healthy life, and wants his readers to share that passion. Their health and well-being comes first. He is anti-dogmatic, and unwavering in his dedication to improve the quality of life of his readers. He has been called "the conscience of modern medicine," a "medical maverick," and has been voted "Doctor of the Year" by the National Health Federation. His medical experiences are far reaching-from battling malaria in Central America - to fighting deadly epidemics at his own health clinic in Africa - to flying with U.S. Navy crews as a flight surgeon - to working for 10 years in emergency medicine here in the States. These learning experiences, not to mention his keen storytelling ability and wit, make Dr. Douglass' newsletters (Daily Dose and Real Health) and books uniquely interesting and fun to read. He shares his no-frills, no-bull approach to health care, often amazing his readers by telling them to ignore many widely-hyped good-health practices (like staying away from red meat, avoiding coffee, and eating like a bird), and start living again by eating REAL food, taking some inexpensive supplements, and doing the pleasurable things that make life livable. Readers get all this, plus they learn how to burn fat, prevent cancer, boost libido, and so much more. And, Dr. Douglass is not afraid to challenge the latest studies that come out, and share the real story with his readers. Dr. William C. Douglass has led a colorful, rebellious, and crusading life. Not many physicians would dare put their professional reputations on the line as many times as this courageous healer has. A vocal opponent of "business-as-usual" medicine, Dr. Douglass has championed patients' rights and physician commitment to wellness throughout his career. This dedicated physician has repeatedly gone far beyond the call of duty in his work to spread the truth about alternative therapies. For a full year, he endured economic and physical hardship to work with physicians at the Pasteur Institute in St. Petersburg, Russia, where advanced research on photoluminescence was being conducted. Dr. Douglass comes from a distinguished family of physicians. He is the fourth generation Douglass to practice medicine, and his son is also a physician. Dr. Douglass graduated from the University of Rochester, the Miami School of Medicine, and the Naval School of Aviation and Space Medicine.

You want to protect those you love from the health dangers the authorities aren't telling you about, and learn the incredible cures that they've scorned and ignored?
Subscribe to the free Daily Dose updates "...the straight scoop about health, medicine, and politics." by sending an e-mail to real_sub@agoramail.net with the word "subscribe" in the subject line.

Dr. William Campbell Douglass'
Real Health:

Had Enough?

Enough turkey burgers and sprouts?

Enough forcing gallons of water down your throat?

Enough exercising until you can barely breathe?

Before you give up everything just because "everyone" says it's healthy...

Learn the facts from Dr. William Campbell Douglass, medicine's most acclaimed myth-buster. In every issue of Dr. Douglass' Real Health newsletter, you'll learn shocking truths about "junk medicine" and how to stay healthy while eating eggs, meat and other foods you love.

With the tips you'll receive from Real Health, you'll see your doctor less, spend a lot less money and be happier and healthier while you're at it. The road to Real Health is actually easier, cheaper and more pleasant than you dared to dream.

Subscribe to Real Health today by calling 1-800-981-7162 or visit the Real Health web site at www.realhealthnews.com.
Use promotional code : DRHBDZZZ

If you knew of a procedure that could save thousands maybe millions, of people dying from AIDS, cancer, and other dreaded killers....

Would you cover it up?

It's unthinkable that what could be the best solution ever to stopping the world's killer diseases is being ignored, scorned, and rejected. But that is exactly what's happening right now.

The procedure is called "photoluminescence". It's a thoroughly tested, proven therapy that uses the healing power of the light to perform almost miraculous cures.

This remarkable treatment works its incredible cures by stimulating the body's own immune responses. That's why it cures so many ailments--and why it's been especially effective against AIDS! Yet, 50 years ago, it virtually disappeared from the halls of medicine.

Why has this incredible cure been ignored by the medical authorities of this country? You'll find the shocking answer here in the pages of this new edition of Into the Light. Now available with the blood irradiation Instrument Diagram and a complete set of instructions for building your own "Treatment Device". Also includes details on how to use this unique medical instrument.

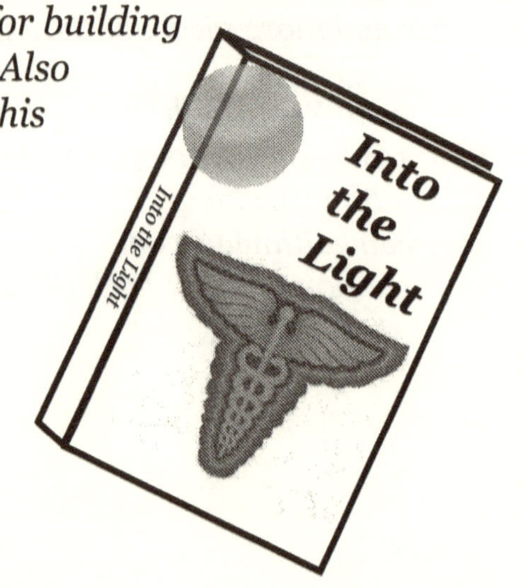

Dr. Douglass' Complete Guide to Better Vision

A report about eyesight and what can be done to improve it naturally. But I've also included information about how the eye works, brief descriptions of various common eye conditions, traditional remedies to eye problems, and a few simple suggestions that may help you maintain your eyesight for years to come.
-William Campbell Douglass II, MD

The Hypertension Report.
Say Good Bye to High Blood Pressure.

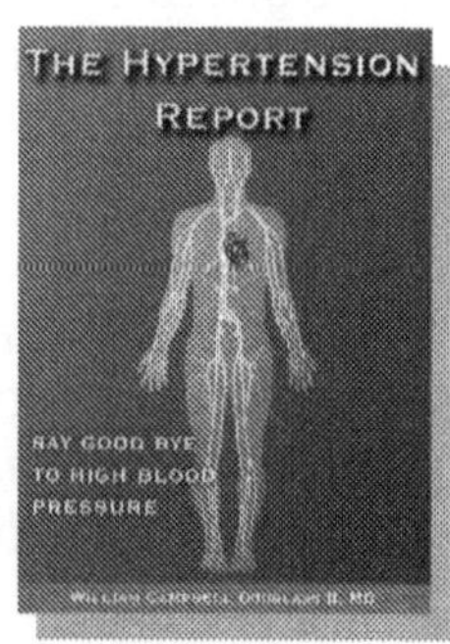

An estimated 50 million Americans have high blood pressure. Often called the "silent killer" because it may not cause symptoms until the patient has suffered serious damage to the arterial system. Diet, exercise, potassium supplements chelation therapy and practically anything but drugs is the way to go and alternatives are discussed in this report.

Grandma Bell's A To Z Guide To Healing With Herbs.

This book is all about - coming home. What I once believed to be old wives' tales - stories long destroyed by the new world of science - actually proved to be the best treatment for many of the common ailments you and I suffer through. So I put a few of them together in this book with the sincere hope that Grandma Bell's wisdom will help you recover your common sense, and take responsibility for your own health. -William Campbell Douglass II, MD

Prostate Problems:
Safe, Simple, Effective Relief for Men over 50.

Don't be frightened into surgery or drugs you may not need. First, get the facts about prostate problems... know all your options, so you can make the best decisions. This fully documented report explains the dangers of conventional treatments, and gives you alternatives that could save you more than just money!

What Is Going on Here?

Peroxides are supposed to be bad for you. Free radicals and all that. But now we hear that hydrogen peroxide is good for us. Hydrogen peroxide will put extra oxygen in your blood. There's no doubt about that. Hydrogen peroxide costs pennies. So if you can get oxygen into the blood cheaply and safely, maybe cancer (which doesn't like oxygen), emphysema, AIDS, and many other terrible diseases can be treated effectively. Intravenous hydrogen peroxide rapidly relieves allergic reactions, influenza symptoms, and acute viral infections.

No one expects to live forever. But we would all like to have a George Burns finish. The prospect of finishing life in a nursing home after abandoning your tricycle in the mobile home park is not appealing. Then comes the loss of control of vital functions the ultimate humiliation. Is life supposed to be from tricycle to tricycle and diaper to diaper? You come into this world crying, but do you have to leave crying? I don't believe you do. And you won't either after you see the evidence. Sounds too good to be true, doesn't it? Read on and decide for yourself.

-William Campbell Douglass II, MD

Don't drink your milk!

If you knew what we know about milk... BLEECHT! All that pasteurization, homogenization and processing is not only cooking all the nutrients right out of your favorite drink. It's also adding toxic levels of vitamin D.

This fascinating book tells the whole story about milk. How it once was nature's perfect food...how "raw," unprocessed milk can heal and boost your immune system ... why you can't buy it legally in this country anymore, and what we could do to change that.

Dr. "Douglass traveled all over the world, tasting all kinds of milk from all kinds of cows, poring over dusty research books in ancient libraries far from home, to write this light-hearted but scientifically sound book.

Rhino Publishing, S.A.
www.rhinopublish.com

Eat Your Cholesterol!

Eat Meat, Drink Milk, Spread The Butter- And Live Longer!
How to Live off the Fat of the Land and Feel Great.

Americans are being saturated with anti-cholesterol propaganda. If you watch very much television, you're probably one of the millions of Americans who now has a terminal case of cholesterol phobia. The propaganda is relentless and is often designed to produce fear and loathing of this worst of all food contaminants. You never hear the food propagandists bragging about their product being fluoride-free or aluminum-free, two of our truly serious food-additive problems. But cholesterol, an essential nutrient, not proven to be harmful in any quantity, is constantly pilloried as a menace to your health. If you don't use corn oil, Fleischmann's margarine, and Egg Beaters, you're going straight to atherosclerosis hell with stroke, heart attack, and premature aging -- and so are your kids. Never feel guilty about what you eat again! Dr. Douglass shows you why red meat, eggs, and dairy products aren't the dietary demons we're told they are. But beware: This scientifically sound report goes against all the "common wisdom" about the foods you should eat. Read with an open mind.

Rhino Publishing, S.A.
www.rhinopublish.com

The Joy of Mature Sex
and How to Be a Better Lover

Humans are very confused about what makes good sex. But I believe humans have more to offer each other than this total licentiousness common among animals. We're talking about mature sex. The kind of sex that made this country great.

Stop Aging or Slow the Process
How Exercise With Oxygen Therapy
(EWOT) Can Help

EWOT (pronounced ee-watt) stands for Exercise With Oxygen Therapy. This method of prolonging your life is so simple and you can do it at home at a minimal cost. When your cells don't get enough oxygen, they degenerate and die and so you degenerate and die. It's as simple as that.

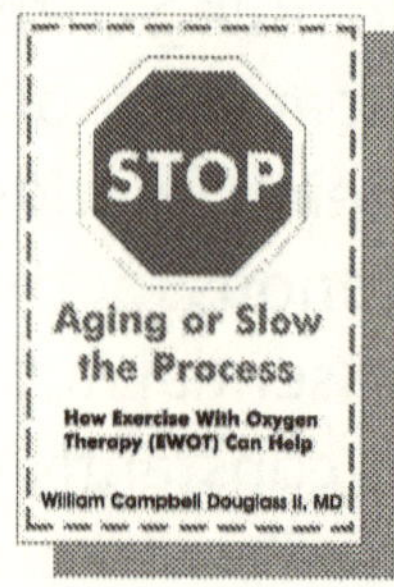

Hormone Replacement Therapies:
Astonishing Results For Men And Women

It is accurate to say that when the endocrine glands start to fail, you start to die. We are facing a sea change in longevity and health in the elderly. Now, with the proper supplemental hormones, we can slow the aging process and, in many cases, reverse some of the signs and symptoms of aging.

Add 10 Years to Your Life
With some "best of" Dr. Douglass' writings.

To add ten years to your life, you need to have the right attitude about health and an understanding of the health industry and what it's feeding you. Following the established line on many health issues could make you very sick or worse! Achieve dynamic health with this collection of some of the "best of" Dr. Douglass' newsletters.

PAINFUL DILEMMA

Are we fighting the wrong war?

We are spending millions on the war against drugs while we
should be fighting the war against pain with those drugs!

As you will read in this book, the war on drugs was lost a long time ago and,
when it comes to the war against pain, pain is winning! An article in USA Today
(11/20/02) reveals that dying patients are not getting relief from pain. It seems
the doctors are torn between fear of the government, certainly justified, and a
clinging to old and out dated ideas about pain, which is NOT justified.

A group called Last Acts, a coalition of health-care groups, has released a very
discouraging study of all 50 states that nearly half of the 1.6 million Americans
living in nursing homes suffer from untreated pain. They said that life was being
extended but it amounted to little more than "extended pain and suffering."

This book offers insight into the history of pain treatment and the current failed
philosophies of contemporary medicine. Plus it describes some of today's most
advanced treatments for alleviating certain kinds of pain. This book is not another
"self-help" book touting home remedies; rather, Painful Dilemma: Patients in
Pain -- People in Prison, takes a hard look at where we've gone wrong and what
we (you) can do to help a loved one who is living with chronic pain.

The second half of this book is a must read if you value your freedom. We now
have the ridiculous and tragic situation of people
in pain living in a government-created hell by
restriction of narcotics and people in prison for
trying to bring pain relief by the selling of
narcotics to the suffering. The end result of the
"war on drugs" has been to create the greatest
and most destructive cartel in history, so great,
in fact, that the drug Mafia now controls most
of the world economy.

Live the Adventure!

Why would anyone in their right mind put everything they own in storage and move to Russia, of all places?! But when   maverick physician Bill Douglass left a profitable medical practice in a peaceful mountaintop town to pursue "pure medical truth".... none of us who know him well was really surprised.

After All, anyone who's braved the outermost reaches of darkest Africa, the mean streets of Johannesburg and New York, and even a trip to Washington to testify before the Senate, wouldn't bat and eye at ducking behind the Iron Curtain for a little medical reconnaissance!

Enjoy this imaginative, funny, dedicated man's tales of wonder and woe as he treks through a year in St. Petersburg, working on a cure for the world's killer diseases. We promise --

YOU WON'T BE BORED!

Rhino Publishing S.A.
www.rhinopublish.com

THE SMOKER'S PARADOX
THE HEALTH BENEFITS OF TOBACCO!

The benefits of smoking tobacco have been common knowledge for centuries. From sharpening mental acuity to maintaining optimal weight, the relatively small risks of smoking have always been outweighed by the substantial improvement to mental and physical health. Hysterical attacks on tobacco notwithstanding, smokers always weigh the good against the bad and puff away or quit according to their personal preferences. Now the same anti-tobacco enterprise that has spent billions demonizing the pleasure of smoking is providing additional reasons to smoke. Alzheimer's, Parkinson's, Tourette's Syndrome, even schizophrenia and cocaine addiction are disorders that are alleviated by tobacco. Add in the still inconclusive indication that tobacco helps to prevent colon and prostate cancer and the endorsement for smoking tobacco by the medical establishment is good news for smokers and non-smokers alike. Of course the revelation that tobacco is good for you is ruined by the pharmaceutical industry's plan to substitute the natural and relatively inexpensive tobacco plant with their overpriced and ineffective nicotine substitutions. Still, when all is said and done, the positive revelations regarding tobacco are very good reasons indeed to keep lighting those cigars - but only 4 a day!

Rhino Publishing, S.A
www.rhinopublish.com

Bad Medicine
How Individuals Get Killed By Bad Medicine.

Do you really need that new prescription or that overnight stay in the hospital? In this report, Dr. Douglass reveals the common medical practices and misconceptions endangering your health. Best of all, he tells you the pointed (but very revealing!) questions your doctor prays you never ask. Interesting medical facts about popular remedies are revealed.

Dangerous Legal Drugs
The Poisons in Your Medicine Chest.

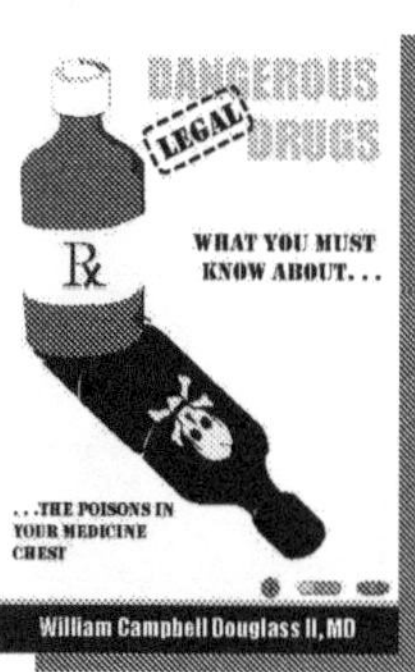

If you knew what we know about the most popular prescription and over-the-counter drugs, you'd be sick. That's why Dr. Douglass wrote this shocking report about the poisons in your medicine chest. He gives you the low-down on different categories of drugs. Everything from painkillers and cold remedies to tranquilizers and powerful cancer drugs.

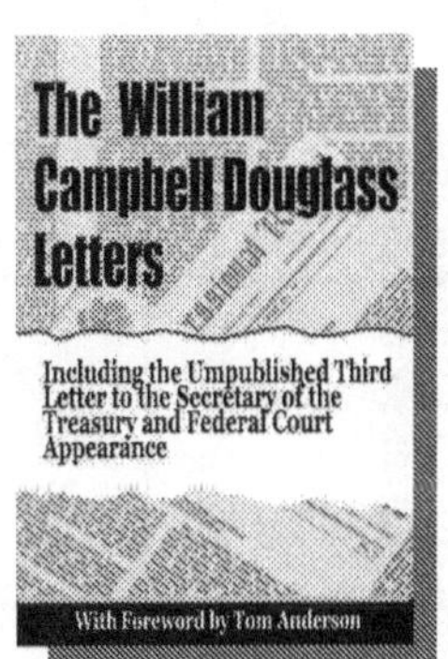

The William Campbell Douglass Letters.
Expose of Government Machinations
(Vietnam War).

THE WILLIAM CAMPBELL DOUGLASS LETTERS. Dr. Douglass' Defense in 1968 Tax Case and Expose of Government Machinations during the Vietnam War.

The Eagle's Feather. A Novel of
International Political Intrigue.

Although The Eagle's Feather is a work of fiction set in the 1970's, it is built, as with most fiction, on a framework of plausibility and background information. This is a fiction book that could not have been written were it not for various ominous aspects, which pose a clear and present danger to the security of the United States.

Rhino Publishing

ORDER FORM

PURCHASER INFORMATION

Purchaser's Name (Please Print): ____________________

Shipping Address (Do not use a P.O. Box): ____________________

City: ____________ State/Prov.: ____________ Country: ____________

Zip/Postal Code: __________ Telephone No.: ____________ Fax No.: ____________

E-Mail Address (if interested in receiving free e-Books when available): ____________________

CREDIT CARD INFO (CIRCLE ONE):
MASTERCARD, VISA, AMERICAN EXPRESS, DISCOVER, JCB, DINER'S CLUB, CARTE BLANCHE.

Charge my Card -> Number #: ____________________ Exp.: __________

***Security Code:** __________ * Required for all MasterCard, Visa and American Express purchases. For your security, we require that you enter your card's verification number. The verification number is also called a CCV number. This code is the 3 digits farthest right in the signature field on the back of your VISA/MC, or the 4 digits to the right on the front of your American Express card. Your credit card statement will show **a different name than Rhino Publishing** as the vendor.

WE DO NOT share your private information, we use 3rd party credit card processing service to process your order only.

ADDITIONAL INFORMATION

If your shipping address is not the same as your credit card billing address, please indicate your card billing address here.

______________________________ Type of card: ______________________________
Name on the card

Billing Address:______________________________

City: _______________ State/Prov.: _______________ Zip/Postal Code: _______________

Fax a copy of this order to:
RHINO PUBLISHING, S.A.
1-888-317-6767 or International #: + 416-352-5126

To order by mail, send your payment by first class mail only to the following address. Please include a copy of this order form. Make your check or bank drafts (NO postal money order) payable to RHINO PUBLISHING, S.A. and mail to:

Rhino Publishing, S.A.
Attention: PTY 5048
P.O. Box 025724
Miami, FL.
USA 33102

Digital E-books also available online: www.rhinopublish.com

Rhino Publishing

ORDER FORM

Purchaser's Name (Please Print): ___________________________

I would like to order the following paperback book of Dr. Douglass (Alternative Medicine Books):

___	X	9962-636-04-3	Add 10 Years to Your Life. With some "best of" Dr. Douglass writings.	$13.99 $______
___	X	9962-636-07-8	AIDS and Biological Warfare. What They Are Not Telling You!	$17.99 $______
___	X	9962-636-09-4	Bad Medicine. How Individuals Get Killed By Bad Medicine.	$11.99 $______
___	X	9962-636-10-8	Color Me Healthy. The Healing Power of Colors.	$11.99 $______
___	X	9962-636 -XX-X	Color Filters for Color Me Healthy. 11 Basic Roscolene Filters for Lamps.	$21.89 $______
___	X	9962-636-15-9	Dangerous Legal Drugs. The Poisons in Your Medicine Chest.	$13.99 $______
___	X	9962-636-18-3	Dr. Douglass' Complete Guide to Better Vision. Improve eyesight naturally.	$11.99 $______
___	X	9962-636-19-1	Eat Your Cholesterol! How to Live off the Fat of the Land and Feel Great.	$11.99 $______
___	X	9962-636-12-4	Grandma Bell's A To Z Guide To Healing. Her Kitchen Cabinet Cures.	$14.99 $______
___	X	9962-636-22-1	Hormone Replacement Therapies. Astonishing Results For Men & Women	$11.99 $______
___	X	9962-636-25-6	Hydrogen Peroxide: One of the Most Underused Medical Miracle.	$15.99 $______
___	X	9962-636-27-2	Into the Light. New Edition with Blood Irradiation Instrument Instructions.	$19.99 $______
___	X	9962-636-54-X	Milk Book. The Classic on the Nutrition of Milk and How to Benefit from it.	$17.99 $______

__	X	9962-636-00-0	Painful Dilemma - Patients in Pain - People in Prison.	$17.99	$______
___	X	9962-636-32-9	Prostate Problems. Safe, Simple, Effective Relief for Men over 50.	$11.99	$______
___	X	9962-636-34-5	St. Petersburg Nights. Enlightening Story of Life and Science in Russia.	$17.99	$______
___	X	9962-636-37-X	Stop Aging or Slow the Process. Exercise With Oxygen Therapy Can Help.	$11.99	$______
___	X	9962-636-60-4	The Hypertension Report. Say Good Bye to High Blood Pressure.	$11.99	$______
___	X	9962-636-48-5	The Joy of Mature Sex and How to Be a Better Lover...	$13.99	$______
___	X	9962-636-43-4	The Smoker's Paradox: Health Benefits of Tobacco.	$14.99	$______

Political Books:

___	X	9962-636-40-X	The Eagle's Feather. A 70's Novel of International Political Intrigue.	$15.99	$______
___	X	9962-636-46-9	The W. C. D. Letters. Expose of Government Machinations (Vietnam War).	$11.99	$______
				SUB-TOTAL:	$______

	ADD $5.00 HANDLING FOR YOUR ORDER:		$ 5.00	$ 5.00
___ X	ADD $2.50 SHIPPING FOR EACH ITEM ON ORDER:		$ 2.50	$______
	NOTE THAT THE MINIMUM SHIPPING AND HANDLING IS $7.50 FOR 1 BOOK ($5.00 + $2.50)			
	For order shipped outside the US. add $5.00 per item			
___ X	ADD $5.00 S. & H. OR EACH ITEM ON ORDER (INTERNATIONAL ORDERS ONLY)		$ 5.00	$______
	Allow up to 21 days for delivery (we will call you about back orders if any)			
			TOTAL:	$______

Fax a copy of this order to: 1-888-317-6767 or Int'l + 416-352-5126
or mail to: Rhino Publishing, S.A. Attention: PTY 5048 P.O. Box 025724, Miami, FL., 33102 USA
Digital E-books also available online: www.rhinopublish.com